MURDER IN PROTOCOL

ANNE CLEELAND

ARTEMIS
—PRESS—

THE DOYLE & ACTON MYSTERY SERIES IN ORDER:

For King Raedwald, who was long-forgot; and for all others like him.

CHAPTER 1

"Vengeance there will be, whether sooner or later. The longer the vengeance is drawn out, the more satisfying it will be."

—Viking quote from Ljósvetninga Saga,
circa 1100 AD

Kathleen Doyle was a seasoned police officer, a notable homicide detective, and the recipient of no less than two commendations for bravery from Scotland Yard, but when it came to speaking in public, bravery was something in very short order.

At present, she was giving a speech at St. Brigid's School for Girls where she'd attended primary school in Dublin; she and her husband were donating a science lab to the school, and—as could be expected—the Mother Superior had asked if Doyle could say a few words at the groundbreaking ceremony.

A portion of the school's orchard was being sacrificed for the new building—space being at a premium, here in the older part of town—and they'd cleared out many of the trees, being as they were quite old, and not very fruitful in the first place.

Doyle had practiced her speech the night before with Acton, her husband, who now sat in the front row at the outdoor ceremony so as to give her silent encouragement. It was a shame that he wasn't the one giving the speech; he was well-used to saying just the right thing being as he was an aristocrat, and the nobs were all born with an extra dose of flim-flam.

Doyle cleared her throat and began, "Good mornin', everyone. My old teachers must be that surprised that I'm the one who's dedicatin' a science lab."

Acton had suggested that she start out with something humorous, and the assembled audience smiled and chuckled—save for the students, who were fidgeting in their seats the same way she'd done when forced to make nice to the benefactors. Doyle herself had been a mediocre student—barely managing to make passing grades—and on top of that, she'd been shy and withdrawn due to two important factors; the first being that she was the only girl at the school without a father—he'd abandoned her mother shortly after she was born—and the second being that she was what the Irish would call "fey"; born with an extraordinary perceptive ability which was something of a mixed blessing, truth to tell, and made for an isolated existence. It was no easy thing, to sense the cross-currents of emotion that surrounded her when she was amongst other people, and so she'd been content to remain an outsider—alongside her mother, who was also an outsider—and the two of them had managed a happy existence together, even after they'd moved to London so that Doyle could pursue a police career.

Unfortunately, her mother had died shortly after the move, and therefore Doyle had found herself living an even more isolated existence as a stranger in a strange land—until that fateful morning when she'd been paired-up on a work assignment with the renowned Chief Inspector Acton, and the man had subsequently decided he'd best marry her, so as to thoroughly upend her carefully isolated little world.

And so now here she was, back at St. Brigid's in a prodigal-daughter sort of story after marrying an English aristocrat with far too much money so as to allow her to dedicate a science lab even though she should thank God fastin' there wasn't a science lab here when she was a student. Ironic, it all was.

Realizing that she was allowing her mind to wander—stay focused, and finish this up, for the love o' Mike—she continued, "It is my and my husband's—" Faith, that wasn't right, and she corrected it to, "It is our hope that this new facility will lead to many careers in science for the students."

"Hear, hear," called out Robbie O'Shaughnessy, being cheeky from his seat in the teacher's section. He was a former copper who'd grown up with Doyle's mother, and was now a mathematics teacher at the school.

Again, everyone chuckled and Doyle relaxed a bit; she was amongst friends here—or at least, if they weren't friends they were supporters, being as the nuns who used to despair of teaching Doyle her sums were now the lucky recipients of large sums of money from the English lord that Doyle had somehow managed to marry. And as a direct result of her husband's devotion to his unlikely wife, the school would now have a new science lab, alongside the other various facilities that the House of Acton had donated.

"I have many happy memories of my time, here—" this wasn't

exactly true, but Acton had explained it was something she should say, regardless "—and I truly hope to hear more of my happy memories—" No, that wasn't right "—I hope many more memories will be made. Happy ones, I mean."

There was an awkward moment of silence, and she could feel her color rising as she reviewed her note cards—she'd missed the part where she was supposed to thank the Mother Superior for her introduction—faith, she'd mucked it up, but best carry on.

She found her place with a firm finger and then lifted her face to the audience again, but found that her gaze strayed over their heads to the trees that still remained on the perimeter of this orchard; the trees had been planted by the founders, way-back-when, and the present Committee had decided that a few of them should remain, for continuity's sake.

As she reviewed the gnarled, ancient trees, she was somewhat surprised to see that a man stood amongst them. And not just any man; this one pinged her copper-radar, mainly because he looked to be a blackleg if she'd ever seen one; a rough-looking fellow with a shaved head and tattoos all along the sides of his face. Strange, that security had allowed him in to watch the ceremony, but it was possible he was one of the invited guests at this little holy-show—you never knew, nowadays, and to each his own. Besides, he seemed harmless—seemed heartily amused by it all, grinning at her as though he found her hilarious.

Dragging her gaze away from the strange man, she focused again on the faces before her, and found that she'd a sudden desire to go off-script. "I've always loved the trees in this orchard," she confessed. "And it seems a crackin' shame we've had to tear most of them down, but I think the cause is a worthy one. This science lab will produce a different sort of first-fruits— God willin'—since we'll build it with the same hopeful spirit as the people who planted the orchard originally; hope that the seeds we plant will grow into blessings for the generations to come—blessings some of us may never witness ourselves."

There was a small silence, and even the students stopped fidgeting as Doyle knit her brow. "When you think about it, in the founders' time, plantin' the orchard was a huge step of faith—here in the midst of a crowded, smoky city, and with no hope to see fruit for many years. And now, it's the trees' turn to give way for the next step of faith. I suppose one day it will be time to replace the science lab with somethin' even more beneficial to the students who will walk the halls here—someday, far into the future. The things that are important to us won't be the things that are important to them, and so the things we've planted may have to be uprooted, to suit the times. I suppose you could say that history's always movin' forward, and doesn't much care how much we'd like to cling to the past, or how much we'd like things to stay just the way they are."

She paused, thinking about this. "No matter what comes next, though, the spirit remains the same—a spirit of lookin' forward with hope, for blessings to come. That's the one thing that never changes."

And then, since she'd already gone off-script and wasn't sure what to say next, she concluded, "Amen."

With some gratification, she heard a sincere round of applause, even as she realized she'd forgot to thank her husband and the Committee—ah, well; they knew what they'd accomplished, so there was no need to gild the lily.

"Well said," Sister Mary Theresa murmured as she came to the podium, surreptitiously bringing a heavy sleeve to dab at her eye. "Very moving."

"Thanks," said Doyle, who decided that there was truly nothing to this public-speaking business, after all.

The Mother Superior's Second—Sister Cecilia—then handed Doyle the ceremonial spade to break ground, and they all moved toward the area that had been roped-off for this time-honored ritual.

"Lord Acton," Sister Mary Theresa indicated Doyle's husband with a gracious gesture; "if you would join us for the photographs?" This, because the school's transformation would not have been possible save for the House of Acton's willingness to open its coffers; ironically, the luckiest thing that ever happened to the struggling little Irish school was that one of its former students happened to catch her commanding officer's eye at far-away Scotland Yard. It was an unlikely Cinderella story, but then again, that was the always the charm of such a story—that it was so very unlikely.

The ground-breaking party assembled for their photograph, with Robbie O'Shaughnessy importantly directing them as to where they should stand, since he was the designated picture-taker. "Right then—everyone hold still, and I'll take a snap," he instructed, and Doyle dutifully held the spade at the ready whilst everyone paused for the photo.

Pinning on her publicity-photo smile—a shame that she had one, and was called-upon to display it so often—Doyle stood beside her husband as the moment was recorded for posterity, the photos slated to be displayed in the archive-gallery that lined the main hallway of the school. It was a strange feeling, to think her own photo would be added to the collection of old photos that she'd walked past every day without paying the slightest attention. It made you rather think that God had a mighty sense of humor, and was enjoying Himself immensely.

But her pinned-on smile suddenly froze, as she stood in shocked disbelief. "Mother a' Mercy," she breathed.

"What is it?" Acton asked quietly, bending to bring his head closer to hers "Are you all right?"

"Only one more snap, Lord Acton," Robbie cautioned, as he held up a finger. "Please stay still."

"Michael," Doyle said in an urgent whisper; "there's a code-eighteen under here."

She could sense his abject surprise, and small blame to him; a code-eighteen was a dead body.

"Are you certain?" he asked in a low voice.

"Aye. Just beneath where I'm supposed to dig."

He paused, because this revelation created an immediate dilemma; few knew about Doyle's perceptive abilities—with good reason, of course—and her husband was very protective of her when it came to such things; one could only imagine the firestorm that would erupt if the man's wedded wife was shown to have strange and unquantifiable powers.

"Dig," he directed quietly. "I will handle it."

Bracing herself, Doyle cautiously plied the spade into the dirt, and then turned over a shovelful to scattered applause and yet another wretched photo.

"Hold," Acton said in a loud voice, as he reached to stay the spade. "I believe I smell decomp."

O'Shaughnessy—the former policeman—stepped forward like a hound to the point. "Where? Here?"

"Yes," said Acton, crouching down, and scrutinizing the area where the soil had been overturned. "Just here. It may only be an animal."

"Everybody back," the other man directed importantly. "We may have a crime scene."

"Goodness me," said Sister Mary Theresa, thoroughly astonished.

Acton took the spade from Doyle's hand and said to O'Shaughnessy, "Let's take a look—if you would give me a hand."

"Certainly, sir."

"I think I saw the perp," Doyle whispered urgently into Acton's ear. "Should we call for back-up?"

"Not as yet," he replied in the same low tone—which only made sense, since they hadn't yet recovered a body—first things first.

O'Shaughnessy was carefully scraping away dirt whilst Acton plied the shovel, and when they'd gone down about eighteen inches, the other man announced with some excitement, "Here's somethin'."

And indeed, it was. As more dirt was brushed aside, Doyle was not over-surprised to see whitened objects, and—after more brushing-away—those objects were revealed to be the bones of a human hand, spread out atop some sort of rough canvas material.

"Merciful heaven," Sister Cecilia breathed, as she and Sister Mary Theresa solemnly made the Sign of the Cross—Doyle belatedly following suit.

"If you would call the local Garda, please," Acton said to them. "And clear the area; we will need to secure the site."

"Of course," the Mother Superior agreed with a brisk nod. She then signaled to the ushers to help her disperse the crowd.

O'Shaughnessy kept brushing away at the soil—the protocols would require that they wait for the Coroner, but Doyle could scarce blame the man; she was agog, herself, and good luck holding back a copper when he was hot on the trail.

With some excitement, the other man glanced up at Acton. "Well, well; will you look at that?"

"Indeed," Doyle's husband replied. Enough dirt had been brushed aside to reveal a human skull, the dome intact, save for a inches-long slot where a sharp instrument had pierced it.

"If you would alert Homicide, please," Acton said.

CHAPTER 2

*I*t was something of a surprise for Doyle to meet the
Garda's Superintendent, and discover that the head of
the local police force was already acquainted with Acton—which
was a nice way of saying that the two men didn't like each other
much. On second thought, however, this truly shouldn't have
been much of a surprise, since the last time they'd visited Dublin
it was made fairly clear that the Irish police weren't huge fans of
English aristocrats, especially those who were known to be big
hats from Scotland Yard.

And here we go, she thought with resignation, as she watched
the two senior officers spar politely with one another. Acton's not
used to not being the lead, and this fellow's not going to defer to
him in the slightest. It doesn't help matters, of course, that the
Superintendent's Pakistani, and therefore nurses a few historical
grudges against lordly English-types; he's a bit bristly, and—being
as I'm an Irishwoman, myself—I suppose I can hardly blame him.
Ironic, it is, that hard on the heels of my fine speech, I'm presented

with a situation where history hasn't moved on a'tall, and let this be a lesson.

They were still on-site at the school, watching the Coroner's team carefully excavate the decedent, whose bones looked to belong to a man in his thirties or thereabouts—although some of his teeth were missing; he may have been homeless or otherwise not invested in personal hygiene. Aside from the obvious trauma to the skull, they'd discovered that the decedent had the remnants of a rope 'round his neck for good measure; someone had wanted this poor fellow good and dead.

Doyle had given the Superintendent a description of the potential suspect that she'd seen standing amongst the trees, and they hoped to hear soon from the field-officers who were poring through the CCTV tape, looking for a good image to send 'round to the local Gardas. She'd described the suspect's rather ferocious appearance and the way he'd seemed amused, which was also significant; some killers very much enjoyed revisiting the scene of their misdeeds, and so the man's attitude only cemented his standing as a suspect.

Thus far, however, they'd heard nothing back, which was somewhat surprising; the man she'd seen should have been easy to spot, on the residential streets which surrounded the school.

Whilst they waited, Acton and the Superintendent continued to politely pull caps, and it would all be rather amusing if it weren't a bit embarrassing; Acton was an English nob and the Superintendent was discreet-Pakistani, so their mutual animosity took the form of being over-polite to one another—a strange and unnatural sight here in Ireland, where brawling was a national pastime.

"Chief Inspector," the Pakistani man asked in his precise voice.

"Is it possible that this matter is connected to the other matter that you previously raised with me?"

"No; it is not," Acton replied, his tone a bit clipped.

Well, this is interesting, Doyle thought; this fellow is speaking sideways—doesn't want the likes of me to figure out what he's referring to, which doesn't bode well. It seems that my husband is keeping the wife of his bosom in the dark about something, and the last needful thing is for the aforesaid wife to start having flashbacks to their last visit to Dublin, when Acton had been kept very busy trying to keep her in the dark about multiple unfolding disasters.

Therefore, she wasn't much surprised when her wedded husband deftly changed the subject. "Would you mind if I access the CCTV feed, Superintendent?" he asked, with a tinge of impatience. "It is important that we obtain an image as quickly as possible."

"My officers are very adept at scrutinizing the surveillance tape," the other man insisted, nettled. "There is no need for your assistance, Chief Inspector."

Doyle resisted any impulse to act as mediator, being as the Superintendent was a stickler for protocol and had already scolded O'Shaughnessy for mucking about in the crime scene when he should have waited for the Coroner. She'd no jurisdiction here—neither did Acton, for that matter; instead they'd been cast into an unfamiliar role as witnesses to a potential crime scene—although they'd been witnesses once before, when Father Clarence had turned-up dead at Acton's estate. The police in that case had interviewed them, but decided it wasn't a suspicious death since the priest—whilst fairly young—was overweight and over-exerting himself.

Doyle scalp prickled—which was what it did when her

intuition was telling her to pay attention—and she paused in surprise. Surely, this case had nothing whatsoever to do with the Father Clarence case—wasn't even in the same country, for the love o' Mike. Not to mention by the looks of it, this victim was long-dead; Doyle wasn't a forensics expert, but she'd seen enough code-eighteens to know that these particular bones had been here awhile.

Again, her scalp prickled, and she frowned, wondering why it would. For heaven's sake, these poor bones were old—there was nothing earth-shattering about that; although—although mayhap that meant that the ferocious-looking fellow was not truly a suspect, after all. It seemed unlikely that the perp would come to the scene of the crime to watch the show, if the murder was indeed an old one.

Thoughtfully, her gaze rested on her husband, who was pacing a bit, and allowing his frustration to show. Which was another thing that didn't add-up—normally Acton was as cool as the other side of the pillow, but for some reason, he was behaving in a way that would only shore-up the Superintendent's prejudices against him—by bein' all autocratic, and such. With dawning uneasiness, she was again reminded of the last time they'd visited Dublin, when—as it turned out—Acton had embarked on a campaign to deliberately provoke the local authorities with the express purpose of pulling the wool over their eyes.

Doyle closed her own eyes for a brief moment, and thought with some annoyance that it was a crackin' shame, sometimes, that she knew the man so well—or, at least she knew him as well as anyone could. It seemed clear to her that he was performing a part, and that she'd best discover the purpose behind his prickliness; hopefully history wasn't repeating itself, and he wasn't attempting to distract the local authorities from a dismaying spate of vengeance-murders, like on their last holiday here. Please God, amen.

Not that such a thing was beyond the realm of possibility. She'd married her commanding officer at the drop of a hat—he was her CO, after all, and he'd asked her so nicely—and even though she loved the man dearly, she'd discovered rather quickly that there was much more to the illustrious Chief Inspector than met the eye. Small wonder, that he hadn't wanted to embark on any sort of lengthy courtship, but had bundled her off to the altar as-quick-as-a-cat.

By all appearances, Acton was a brilliant detective— mysterious, aristocratic and reclusive—which heady combination only seemed to endear him to the general public, who loved their larger-than-life heroes. But his new-wedded wife soon discovered that all was not what it appeared, and that Acton had a rather formidable dark side that he kept well-hidden. As it turned out, much of the success that he'd had, in solving thorny homicide cases, stemmed directly from the fact that he was something of a vigilante and therefore not afraid to manipulate the evidence to obtain what he considered the proper outcome. And—being as he was an aristocrat from an ancient bloodline—he'd no qualms whatsoever about such high-handed behavior. In truth, the man's ancestors would no doubt heartily approve; Acton was from a long line of people who'd swung their swords with little regard for the proper protocols.

But it was even worse than mere manipulation of the evidence, unfortunately; if Acton decided that the criminal justice system was not going to reach the proper conclusion, he would often take it upon himself to rid the community of bad actors who'd become too slippery for the rule of law. The illustrious Chief Inspector would not hesitate to engage in a spot of murder, if he felt it was called-for.

Having just graduated from the Crime Academy—where she'd been steeped in the careful protocols that existed to constrain the criminal justice system—Doyle was very much dismayed to arrive at these conclusions, and so—over the course of her marriage, thus far—she'd been trying valiantly to get him to mend his ways. It would not end well, if he continued as he was, and indeed, she'd often felt that before her arrival on the scene Acton had been bent on a path of self-destruction. There'd been more than a touch of mayhem, in his early life, and therefore he had his demons, poor man.

Or at least, he'd demons before he'd met his unlikely wife. Those selfsame demons had been beaten back somewhat, mainly because he was very much afraid that she'd abandon ship if he continued as he was. There was no denying that he loved her—loved her, despite how different they were—and his devotion outstripped everything else in his life.

And since Doyle was a staunch RC, she didn't think it was mere happenstance that he'd managed somehow to fall madly in love with the unlikely likes of her. She was perhaps the one person in the world that he was willing to defer to—not to mention that she was uniquely suited to catch him out, in his questionable misdeeds—and therefore, it seemed clear that Acton's redemption —however daunting the task—had been deliberately put on her plate. It couldn't be a coincidence that two such different people had managed to find each other, and that it worked so well.

And—in a strange way—in the course of trying to change his natural inclinations, Acton had changed hers, too. Doyle was not a bold person, but she'd been called-upon to be bold—and more than once—as a direct result of her association with her husband. As a consequence, she was something of a local folk-hero in

London—with her two commendations for bravery—even though she was someone who was much more inclined to lurk on the sidelines, and sink into obscurity.

All in all, she felt that she'd been largely successful in steering her husband toward a better path, and could tentatively congratulate herself on a job well done. It definitely helped matters that they'd two small sons, now, because it went without saying that when you'd little children underfoot you'd a lot less time to brood and mastermind.

Or so she'd thought, anyway. As she watched her husband hover near the Superintendent in silent disapproval, she wondered if mayhap she'd grown a bit less vigilant in her saving-Acton-from-himself duties, due to the aforementioned two small children. Because unless she very much missed her guess, her husband was up to something; up to something, and—as a corker —the man was smoking, again.

Acton had smoked when he was at university, but he'd dropped the habit long ago—or so she'd thought; it had recently come to her attention that he was smoking again, although he was taking great pains to hide this unfortunate fact from her.

It did not bode well; the only other time he'd smoked—in Doyle's marital experience, thus far—was when he'd been masterminding a scheme to take-down an enemy in horrifying fashion. And Doyle knew—in the way that she knew things—that this relapse was no small thing; if Acton was smoking in secret, Katy bar the door.

It was all a bit bewildering, though; *surely* it was a coincidence, that they'd managed to stumble across an old murder, here on holiday? She was certain that Acton's surprise upon the body's discovery was genuine—he'd no idea they were about to dig-up this poor victim. On the other hand, her husband was secretly smoking and taking every opportunity to needle the Garda Superintendent to a fine point; neither one of these things was in keeping, and—based upon past history—it would probably be in the fair Doyle's best interests to discover why this was.

With an inward sigh, she pulled her mobile to phone Miss Cherry, and decided with some resignation that it didn't look as though they were going to take the boyos to feed the ducks any time soon.

CHAPTER 3

*M*iss Cherry was a warm, amiable woman who'd lived all her life in the town by Trestles, which was Acton's hereditary estate. They'd enlisted her as a nanny fairly recently; she'd no prior experience, but Acton had wanted someone they could trust, since they'd had an amazing run of bad luck when it came to nannies.

Doyle was a bit conflicted about having a nanny in the first place—her own mother had rarely strayed from her side—but it was a practicality; she and Acton had an impressive record of solving homicides because they worked so well together—he so clever, and she so intuitive—and therefore it would serve the greater good if she continued her work with London's CID in a part-time capacity. That, and Acton had lived his life surrounded by servants and wasn't of two minds about it, like she was.

When the nanny answered her phone, Doyle explained, "We'll have to cancel the duck-feedin' plan, Miss Cherry—they've found a body in the orchard, here, and so we're havin' somethin' of a

19

busman's holiday; we've got to hang 'round until they release the scene."

"Gracious," the woman replied, understandably alarmed. "Do they know what happened?"

"Not as yet, but it doesn't look to be a recent murder." Struck with a thought, Doyle advised, "If you'd like, I can meet you and the boys over at the school playground—it's on the other side from the orchard, and as long as they stay away from the site I can't see the harm; it's not like Acton and I are the ones workin' this case, so we should be released soon."

Doyle paused in surprise, because—for reasons which were unclear—she'd the sure sense that this was wrong, and that she and Acton were indeed the ones working this case—even though that made little sense. In some confusion, she frowned into her mobile and decided that she *truly* needed to find out why Acton had taken-up smoking again.

"Lady Acton?"

"Oh—oh, yes; let me know when you are on the way—no hurry."

"Very good, ma'am."

Doyle then rang off, and walked over to where her husband was engaged in a low-voiced discussion with the Superintendent, the man listening politely even as Doyle was aware that he was fervently wishing that this annoying London interloper would make himself scarce.

In a bright tone, Doyle asked, "What d'we think we have, here?"

"I am not at liberty to say, Officer Doyle," the Superintendent explained politely. "You are a witness, this time."

"Right," Doyle replied with an apologetic smile. Faith, but he was a stickler for the protocols, this one—normally coppers didn't stand on ceremony with each other, whether on or off-duty.

"I am afraid no image has yet been secured," Acton informed her with just the tiniest hint of censure.

The Superintendent could be seen to press his lips together, briefly. "Indeed. We may ask that you give a description of the suspect to a sketch-artist, Officer Doyle."

Doyle nodded her acquiescence, even though such a thing was becoming more and more unusual; ever since the authorities had put-up wall-to-wall CCTV cameras everywhere, sketch-artists tended to be little-needed.

But Acton immediately protested, "Is it necessary to hold my wife for a sketch-artist? The victim's remains are not fresh, and therefore it seems unlikely that the man she described is connected to the case."

"I've no objection a'tall, Michael," Doyle said in a light tone that nevertheless held a hint of warning that she was not best pleased with this performance, here on her home turf. To the Superintendent, she said "D'you mind if I go meet my boys over at the school playground, just on the other side? You can let me know when I'm needed."

"Certainly," the Superintendent said to the reasonable wife, with a polite little nod.

"Perhaps a field-officer could be assigned to accompany her," Acton suggested, as he gave the other man a significant glance.

In a firm tone, his companion replied, "I do not think it necessary, Chief Inspector."

"We do have our own security," Doyle reminded her husband, even though he was in no need of reminding. "Adrian's goin' to drive them over."

O'Shaughnessy, who'd been shamelessly eavesdropping on the

conversation, offered, "I'll escort you over there, missy—I'd love to see your boyos."

This was not the annoyance it might at first seem, in that Doyle suddenly saw an opportunity to do a bit of probing. "Thanks, Robbie; come along, then."

The Irishman fell into step beside Doyle as they walked 'round the building, and—in the time-honored manner of junior officers everywhere—he immediately offered-up a denigrating opinion about senior command.

"He's a right prig—typical Paki," O'Shaughnessy remarked, and rolled his eyes. "We used to lock horns, back when he was just an Inspector."

Diplomatically, Doyle didn't mention that O'Shaughnessy used to lock horns with all his senior officers on a regular basis, and instead replied with a hint of admonishment, "Now then, Robbie; he's only followin' the rules, and we're all on the same team."

"Not anymore," the retired officer reminded her with a bit of cheek. "I've flown, so I can say whatever I wish."

As this seemed a prime opening, Doyle remarked, "Well, it's clear he's not too happy with Acton, nor he with him—they've that issue." She gave him a knowing look.

O'Shaughnessy immediately took this bait, and offered, "You can't blame your husband, missy. He's that worried about your stalkin' problem."

Doyle blinked. "My *stalkin'* problem?"

"Oh—you don't know, do you? He must not want you to know." He patted her shoulder in a patronizing fashion. "Forget I said."

But this inadvertent revelation only cemented Doyle's certain sense that she needed to start paying close attention to whatever-it-was Acton had up his sleeve; after all, if there was a stalking problem there was little doubt that it was her wedded husband who was doing the stalking. But what was he up to? He was laying the groundwork with the Superintendent with some end in mind—on that point she'd no doubt; but on the other hand, he'd no idea that they were going to stumble across a homicide investigation whilst dedicating the new science-lab. It all made little sense.

After deciding she'd best change the subject, she observed, "Faith, I'm that surprised the man that I saw—whether or not he's truly the perp—isn't comin' up on the school's CCTV, let alone the City's. He was standin' amongst the trees, big as life; nasty-lookin' fellow—didn't fit in a'tall." She knit her brow, thinking about this. "He may have been a code forty-three, by the looks of him." This referred to an altered-state criminal—one that may be dangerous due to excessive drug use, or mental problems.

With some alarm, O'Shaughnessy asked, "Could he be the stalker, d'you think?"

Doyle blinked. "Oh. No, I don't think so."

Which gave her pause, in that she was so certain about this. After all, the strange man had definitely been focused on the fair Doyle as she was making her speech, and seemed to be having a rather inappropriate reaction to the proceedings. But nevertheless, she knew—in the way that she knew things—that he didn't constitute a threat, even though this didn't make a lot of sense; his photo could have been the dictionary definition of a threatening individual. And meanwhile, Acton was apparently worried about something—worried enough to request police protection, save that he wasn't worried—not truly. He was only goading the Superintendent, for reasons unknown.

None of this makes a thimbleful of sense, she thought a bit

crossly; and let this be a lesson that we should never go on holiday, ever. Although to be fair, this trip wasn't a holiday, exactly; instead, they were dedicating the new science-lab which only went to show that virtue was *not* its own reward, no matter what the nuns always told you.

Alarmed by such uncharitable thoughts, she quickly offered-up an apology, and decided to make a conscious effort to adjust her bad attitude. It wasn't going to be easy, in that she'd the sure sense—honed by many similar such occasions—that something was brewing, and brewing big.

CHAPTER 4

*W*hilst she waited with O'Shaughnessy for her boys to make their arrival, Doyle was not a'tall surprised to see her husband emerge from around the corner of the school building so as to head their way. He'd known she was unhappy with how he was behaving, and Acton would want to remedy this situation as promptly as possible; he didn't tolerate it well when she was unhappy with him—which was a good thing, in that having to walk the line with his wife had probably saved half the population of London.

"Ho, Michael," Doyle said easily, since she didn't want O'Shaughnessy to catch wind of a marital dispute; after all, the man was not a pattern-card of discretion.

"Took the first chance to escape, eh, Michael?" The Irishman joked in an over-hearty manner.

Inwardly, Doyle winced because Acton wasn't one who invited familiarity, but—since he was already in her black book—her husband was on his best behavior and refrained from snubbing the man as he made a noncommittal reply.

Unfortunately, O'Shaughnessy immediately compounded his error by pronouncing, "Nothin' like a Paki, to set your back up."

Hoping to save the man from an even more-deserved snub, Doyle joked in mock-exasperation, "You mustn't be so prejudiced, Robbie; faith, you'd think all those years of sensitivity trainin' would have left a mark."

"I tended to tune it out," the Irishman admitted, unashamed. "It was such overkill—year after year. The COs needed to check that box, though."

"A necessary chore," said Acton, the CO.

Quickly realizing that perhaps he should backtrack a bit, the other man offered, "Aye; has to be done, I suppose. They do somethin' similar here at the school, too—a yearly class on sensitivity."

"It seems there is no escape," Acton offered in a benign tone, since he was trying to show his wife that he wasn't such a bad sort, after all.

"Can't duck it, in this day and age," O'Shaughnessy agreed, with a philosophical shrug. "A monumental waste of time, truly."

Acton made no response—instead, he seemed to have chosen to be amused by the man's attitude—and Doyle was relieved; for all his heavy-footing, O'Shaughnessy meant well, and he'd been very helpful to the young Doyle, back when she was a rookie copper.

And Doyle was to soon realize why Acton was amused, because their rental van pulled up, and Adrian came around to open the door for Miss Cherry and their sons. Adrian was Miss Cherry's nephew, and both were of African descent.

O'Shaughnessy had the grace to look a bit embarrassed as the two boys ran pell-mell over to greet them—Edward the eldest, followed by Tommy who was still a toddler, but doggedly following Edward to the best of his abilities. In the manner of children his age, Tommy was excitedly trying to relate some incomprehensible tale to his mum, and Doyle had learned that oftentimes his elder brother was in a better position to translate.

"What's he sayin', Edward?"

"He's saying that Mr. Adrian got lost."

"Just for a moment," Adrian confessed with a smile. "Saved by the GPS."

"'Tis like a rabbit warren, around these streets," O'Shaughnessy offered in a hearty tone, since he wanted to show Doyle that he wasn't such a bad sort, either. "It's one of the oldest areas in the city, and so the streets are higgledy-piggledy."

Doyle introduced the Irishman to Adrian and Miss Cherry, whom he greeted with a fine show of friendliness—not that this will teach the man to hold his tongue, Doyle thought; I think that's not a learnable lesson, in his case.

"Paddycake," Tommy insisted brightly, as he held up his little hands to the Irishman.

"What's this?" asked O'Shaughnessy in surprise.

"Don't ask," Doyle warned.

Adrian chuckled. "I'll take a turn. My aunt taught him a pat-a-cake rhyme, and so now he's obsessed."

Patiently, the young man crouched and held up his hands as Tommy slapped them in an inexpert manner, all the while saying unintelligible sing-song words and beaming in the way of very young children who were pleased as punch that they'd mastered something clever, however tedious it might be to the adults around him.

"I've created a monster," Cherry confessed.

"I'll take a turn," O'Shaughnessy volunteered. "Rather reminds me of 'category'—we used to play when I was a youngster."

"He's not ready for category, Robbie," Doyle advised. "He's not ready for pat-a-cake, as it is."

"Oh—well, I'll learn this one, then," the Irishman offered, since he was still trying to demonstrate his extreme lack of prejudice.

But the game was interrupted due to Edward's having decided that he was going over to the playground, and wherever Edward went, Tommy always followed as fast as his little legs could carry him.

The adults followed them in a slower fashion, with O'Shaughnessy saying to Doyle, "That younger laddie—"

"Tommy," Doyle supplied.

"Tommy is the spit of your mum."

Doyle smiled. "D'you think so? I see Acton in Edward, but I suppose Tommy does have the look of her."

"Aye." He blew out his cheeks. "Takes me back, a bit."

Miss Cherry asked, "Were you acquainted with Lady Acton's mother, Mr. O'Shaughnessy?"

"I was, indeed—my whole life long," he replied, and for a moment, his sadness was palpable.

Into the silence, Doyle offered, "They were old friends—my mother missed Robbie sorely, after we'd moved to London." This was not exactly true, but—similar to the remark about her happy times at the school—it was a kindly sort of lie. O'Shaughnessy had offered to marry Doyle's mother, back when she'd dire need of a husband, but she'd declined his offer because Robbie tended to drink, and would use his fists a bit too much as a result. And even though he'd now mended his ways, Doyle couldn't help but think it a wise decision; they'd been very happy together, just her and her mum. And now she'd children of her own, with her own childhood memories fast being replaced by her children's. The past was past, and there was little point in dwelling on it, as O'Shaughnessy was wont to do.

The Irishman mustered-up a bittersweet smile as they watched the two children race about the playground. "'Tis a grand thing, that she lives on in that boy."

"He'll need some help on the swings," Miss Cherry said in a practical tone. "Come along."

The two moved over toward the swing set, which left Doyle standing alone beside her husband. As they watched Edward scramble to the top of the jungle-gym with alarming speed, Doyle offered, "I understand that I've a stalker. Faith, it takes me back, it does."

Her husband made a sound of frustration as he bent his head. "Not in so many words, and it is unfortunate that such an interpretation has been made. I am only being cautious, Kathleen."

"Aye; so cautious that I've no idea what anyone's talkin' about."

But he tilted his head in mild disagreement. "Certainly, Sir Stephen has been behaving badly."

This gave Doyle pause, because—to be fair this was somewhat true. Sir Stephen was Acton's distant cousin and something of a thorn in his side, having been his original heir before Edward and Tommy put paid to that particular line of succession. As a result, the man was now left with little to show for his connection to the House of Acton, since Doyle's husband was not about to give him so much as a farthing; Sir Stephen had once brought an unsuccessful case before Parliament to try to challenge Acton's right to the title, and Doyle's husband was not what anyone would call the forgive-and-forget type.

Doyle had long-known that Sir Stephen was a nasty weasel—the sort of person who was always trying to put one over, so as to gain an advantage—but because he couldn't hold a candle to Acton in the masterminding-department, all of his weasel-plans tended to come to naught. But matters had taken a rather ominous turn, lately, because—for all of his failings—Sir Stephen had managed to murder an RC priest. He'd murdered a priest, and he'd got clean away with it.

Father Clarence had been befriended by Sir Stephen and Acton's mother, the Dowager Lady Acton—a very strange turn of events, since neither were RC—and as a result, the portly priest had been a regular visitor at the Dower House, located on Acton's estate. Tragically, Father Clarence had died suddenly whilst walking in the fields at Trestles, but since he was overweight and overexerting, the death had been ruled a natural one.

In truth, however, Acton's mother and Sir Stephen had orchestrated the priest's death, hoping to gain a fortune. They'd learned that the rather naïve clergyman hailed from a wealthy family, and had managed to convince him to make their trumped-up charitable foundation his heir. They'd then poisoned the poor man with excess amounts of theobromine—a toxin often found in high-end chocolate—and so when the Coroner discovered elevated levels of the substance, he'd ascribed it to the decedent's eating habits rather than deliberate poisoning.

And all had gone according to plan, save for the fact that Melinda—a neighboring aristocrat, who was long-acquainted with Acton and his family—had overheard the two plotters, and had promptly run her own counter-scheme: Melinda had seduced the priest, and convinced him to marry her in secret. Thus, when the poor man died, Melinda had become a wealthy widow with the Dowager and Sir Stephen's plans lying in ashes and ruin.

Acton had carefully swept the whole matter under the rug, of course. Even though he wasn't fond of his mother—and he was even less fond of Sir Stephen—he was mighty fond of his illustrious heritage, and the ensuing scandal would have been horrendous, with his own mother in the dock as a murderess.

The story did not end there, however. As it turned out, the dead priest had a widowed mother in Yorkshire who was minor aristocracy, herself. Lady Madeline was convinced that her only son's death was the result of foul play, and was therefore hell-bent on seeking justice for him. Since the police near Acton's estate hadn't opened a homicide case, Lady Madeline—who held the potent combination of being both furious and wealthy—had hired private investigators, and those investigators had been relentless; they'd interviewed Sir Stephen, the Dowager, and all the personnel at the Dower House—which was all rather a surprise to Doyle, in that Acton had allowed such a thing. After all, no one was under any compulsion to cooperate, since it wasn't an official police investigation.

But—she'd surmised—he must have decided to allow this intrusion so that it wouldn't look as though he was hiding anything, and also because he'd known that—in the end—there wouldn't be enough evidence for the police to open a case; as a Chief Inspector, no one knew the protocols better than he did.

But the private investigation must have made some inroads nevertheless, because in recent days Sir Stephen had come to meet with Acton at their London flat, the two men engaging in an argument that could be heard through Acton's office door—which only went to show that things must be very uneven, indeed; Acton was not a raised-voices sort of person. And Sir Stephen must have been feeling some heat, to make such a visit in the first place—coming hat-in-hand to seek favors from his hated cousin.

Reminded of all this, Doyle made a face. "'Behavin' badly' is puttin' too kind a gloss on it, husband; I know your hands are tied, but I will say that there's some comfort in knowin' that your wretched cousin is actually squirmin' a bit, and payin' even a small price for his sins. But I don't know why you'd tell our Superintendent that he's any sort of danger to us—he's a coward, at heart."

"I have decided to err on the side of caution," Acton replied rather firmly. "We have first-hand experience that Sir Stephen is unpredictable."

"Well, he's predictable in that he's equal parts awful and hare-brained," Doyle pointed out. "I'd be that surprised if you couldn't block him at every turn."

"Even so," he insisted.

Doyle was suddenly given pause, because her trusty instinct was telling her that she should start paying close attention. For reasons unknown, Acton was behaving very much out-of-character, in airing these private family matters to an unsympathetic Garda police officer. It truly made no sense—particularly because Acton himself was a past-master when it came to security; he'd made a lot of enemies in his line of work, and was therefore very cautious when it came to protecting his family.

So; Acton was behaving out-of-character and in Doyle's experience, whenever her husband was behaving out-of-character she should immediately assume he was up to something that would turn her red hair grey—a sad testament, but there it was; the fact that he was smoking again only seemed to put the stamp on this troubling conclusion.

And—as was her usual m.o. on such occasions—she was careful not to let her wedded husband know that her suspicions had been raised, lest he take even greater pains to cover his tracks in layers of guile. Therefore, with a show of genuine curiosity she asked, "Has Lady Madeline's investigation taken a turn? Is that why the wretched man came to call?"

"Yes," he acknowledged. "As a matter of fact, Ms. Davies will come over to meet with me, and give an update tomorrow. She is somewhat concerned that Lady Madeline may have enough evidence to open a criminal case in Yorkshire."

Doyle blinked. Lisa Davies was the rather ruthless solicitor that Acton had hired to represent the interests of the House of Acton for this investigation, and if she was worried, it seemed likely that there was indeed something to be worried about. "How can the Yorkshire police open a case? The man died at Trestles."

But he explained, "Nonetheless, it would be proper protocol. A homicide is triable in any court in the UK, regardless of where it took place."

This was rather unwelcome news, and Doyle glanced up at him in concern. "Small wonder Davies is worried, then; you might hold sway over your local prosecutors, but presumably Lady Madeline holds sway over her Yorkshire prosecutors. She's lookin' for a home-field advantage."

"Yes—you can see why Sir Stephen is concerned. And there are more Roman Catholics in Yorkshire than near Trestles, certainly. A jury would be immediately prejudiced, given the nature of the crime."

Doyle blew out a breath, as she turned back to watch the children. "Faith, Lady Madeline should try to make him face the music here in Ireland; we'd eat Sir Stephen alive, for killin' a priest."

But her husband only reminded her, "Ireland has an independent criminal apparatus; a homicide case could not be filed here."

"Oh—oh, right," said Doyle hastily, since she should know this, having started her police career in Dublin. "Our rules are separate from the rest of the UK—and ours are a bit more loosey-goosey, besides."

Her scalp started prickling, and she paused in surprise, wondering why it would. It was true that Ireland didn't share a criminal code with the rest of Great Britain—Ireland tended to go its own way, when it came to criminal cases—but why this was important was unclear. After all, it was not as though Sir Stephen had murdered anyone in Ireland—although wouldn't *that* have made Acton cock a' hoop? Nothing he'd like better, one would think, than to pack-off his hated cousin to Maghaberry Prison in Northern Ireland. The notorious, remote prison tended to house only the worst of the worst, and in the past, it had served as a final destination for many of Acton's enemies—whether they actually deserved to go there or not.

Fortunately, the fair Doyle had twigged onto this rather horrifying practice, and had made her husband promise he'd no longer pull strings so as to send-off his enemies to Maghaberry, so that they'd subsequently sink from sight.

Rather dismayed by the direction of her thoughts—and doubly dismayed that her intuition was telling her to pay attention—Doyle ventured, "Well, be that as it may, I'm not sure what you think the Superintendent can do about Sir Stephen. He's not goin' to assign additional protection to the likes of us—that's not the Garda's role—and besides, he's got a budget to worry about."

But her husband explained, "Ordinarily, that may be true,

Kathleen, but there are different protocols for Internationally Protected Persons."

She blinked. "What's that, again?"

"We are Internationally Protected Persons. I am a member of the House of Lords, and therefore I am considered a member of a collegial body charged with governance."

She stared at him, thoroughly confused. "Explain to me what this means, please, and pretend that you're speakin' to Edward so that you have to put it in plain terms."

"If a criminal act is directed at an Internationally Protected Person or his family, it may rise to the level of terrorism, depending on the surrounding circumstances."

She stared at him for a bemused moment, and then couldn't help but smile. "So; you're tryin' to convince the Superintendent that your wretched cousin's a likely terrorist? Good luck with that one, Michael."

With an answering smile, he only replied, "It does strain credulity, but then again, I do not make the rules."

His mild tone made her instantly suspicious, and so she decided to cut to the nub. "What's afoot, my friend? It seems very strange that you're suddenly all about the protocols—you've never met a protocol you didn't sidestep whenever you wished. On the other hand, our Superintendent's knows the protocols back-and-edge, and he's not buyin' whatever you're sellin'. It's very unlikely he's goin' to get his Department involved when a couple of English nobs are havin' a dust-up—not to mention as a Pakistani, he doesn't have a lot of patience for English nobs in the first place. You're intent on needlin' the poor man, and I'd like to know why—you're not a needler by nature." This, because Acton was much more a polite-to-your-face-until-you-suddenly-sink-from-sight sort of person.

Stubbornly, he insisted, "I cannot like having my concerns dismissed out-of-hand."

She made a derisive sound. "Well, that's very high-and-mighty of you. Thanks so much for cementin' everyone's suspicions that I've gone over to the dark side, by marryin' the likes of you."

Since he could see that he was making no progress in unruffling her feathers, her husband drew her to his side, and bent his head to hers in a conciliatory manner. "I will admit that I may have come across as arrogant and demanding, and I am sorry for it. I will ask his pardon, and say no more on the subject."

With a sigh, she put her arm around his waist. "And I'm over-sensitive on that subject—especially here, on my home turf. I'll ask for your pardon, too—I shouldn't scold you like you were Edward."

He squeezed her to him. "You may scold me whenever you wish, Kathleen. I deserved it, certainly."

Marital harmony restored, they stood together, arm-in-arm, and watched the swings soar into the sky. Apparently, O'Shaughnessy had said something amusing to Miss Cherry, because they both started laughing aloud.

Oh-oh, thought Doyle with a sudden pang of dismay; those two rather sound the same, when they laugh.

CHAPTER 5

*O*ne of the Garda's field-officers came around the corner of the school building to inform Doyle that the sketch-artist had arrived, if she would please come with him.

Acton turned to accompany her, but she demurred, "No—stay with the boys, Michael; I'd feel better, since we're bein' all over-cautious, and such."

Not that she was actually worried about any potential threat from Sir Stephen; instead, she was looking to buttonhole the Superintendent and seek a few home-truths without her husband present. She'd been married to Acton long enough to learn a lesson or two in guilefulness, herself.

"Very well; text me when you are finished."

"I will," she agreed. And then—seizing the opportunity to stamp-out yet another potential disaster, she called out to O'Shaughnessy, "Can you come along with me, Robbie? We haven't had much chance to catch up."

The other man willingly left his post at the swings, and as soon as they'd walked out of earshot, Doyle scolded, "Miss Cherry's got a beau at home, and don't you *dare* steal her away." The nanny had been seeing Acton's old friend, Timothy McGonigal, and that poor man had been crossed in love so many times that it was a wonder he hadn't taken up Holy Orders.

"A very nice woman," the Irishman said rather defensively. "I was just bein' friendly, is all."

"Well, be friendly from a distance—I'll not be losin' another nanny to romance."

"Listen to you," he chortled. "A dog in the manger."

Doyle frowned slightly. "I don't think that's the right fable— I've my own romance, so I'm not a dog in the manger. Although I can't believe that I'm the one actually correctin' someone else, for a change."

With a cheeky gleam, her companion offered, "I will say that your husband doesn't much seem the romantic type."

Leave it to O'Shaughnessy, to say such a thing, and she scolded mildly, "I'll not be tellin' tales, Robbie—but know that you're wrong, just the same."

Retrenching, her companion explained, "I only meant that he seems more the practical, efficient type."

Doyle brought to mind the case-in-point that was her wedding day, and found that she couldn't disagree. "We'll compromise, then; he's both romantic *and* efficient."

Her companion nodded, happy to have soothed her. "He definitely knows how to get things done—I'll say that for him. He suggested that the school have a science-lab, and bang—it's all put in train. Even suggested the dedication ceremony date, since he knew you'd already be over here on holiday."

Doyle closed her eyes, briefly. Her wily husband had suggested that they take this holiday because they would be in

Dublin anyway for the dedication ceremony. So; as strange as it seemed, it was apparent that Acton had been angling to be in Dublin—of all places—to accomplish whatever scheme he'd taken-up smoking and needling Superintendents to bring about.

As she walked a few steps, thinking about this, she decided that she'd bet her teeth it had something to do with Sir Stephen; Acton wasn't the type of person who would go out of his way to annoy police brass, but Acton was exactly the type of person who'd go out of his way to satisfy his mighty grudge against Sir Stephen—a grudge that was unrequited, if you could say "unrequited vengeance" the same as you'd say "unrequited love."

So; things were starting to make a bit of sense, finally—after all, in the usual course of things, Acton would never have entertained Sir Stephen at their London flat, let alone engaged in an audible argument with the man. But for whatever reason, he was trying to create an evidence-trail that showed his cousin to be threatening and dangerous, even though such was not necessarily the case—although to be fair, he'd definitely been dangerous for poor Father Clarence, God rest his soul.

And the Father Clarence situation was a golden opportunity for Acton; the priest's murder would give him an excuse to bring down the hammer on his cousin, and it would make complete sense if this was the impetus behind all these unusual goings on— this hasty trip to Dublin, and the elaborate pretense that Sir Stephen was somehow a danger to them.

But this promising theory had one major flaw—one that seemed insurmountable, in her view. As much as Father Clarence's murder gave Acton a golden opportunity to go after Sir Stephen, her husband's hands were tied, in that any move against Sir Stephen would bring down a firestorm of scandal on the

House of Acton, and potentially put Acton's own mother in the dock—Sir Stephen was not one who would go quietly.

So—all things taken into consideration, it could well be that Acton had connived to bring them here to Dublin because it would give him the opportunity to serve-up some Acton-style justice far away from Trestles. That way, mayhap he could hope to contain any scandalous fallout involving his mother, since they'd be far away from the London press. And it would also explain why Acton was working his angle with the Superintendent, and talking-up that "'famous protected persons" argument. He must be thinking that he could use whatever-that-protocol-was to lift his mother off the hook, so to speak, being as his mother was a protected member of his family—he could claim she'd been threatened by his cousin, mayhap?

In any event, she could see the rough outlines of an Acton-plan, and it all seemed to fall into place save for one very important detail; no criminal case could be filed in Ireland based on Father Clarence's murder.

Frowning slightly, she asked O'Shaughnessy, "If a homicide's committed in England, is there *any* way that a case can be brought in Dublin?"

Her companion shook his head. "No, missy. No jurisdiction, here—we've our own ways, and we don't follow the UK rules." This, said with a distinct air of superiority.

"Right," Doyle reluctantly agreed, as she decided that this very promising theory seemed a dead end. "And the UK police wouldn't want to bring a homicide case in Ireland anyways, because our protocols tend to be so different—we're a long sight more loosey-goosey."

"Especially for terrorism," he agreed. "There's a lot of controversy, about how our terrorism laws are so much looser than the UK ones, but we had to crack down hard, back in the day."

Since it seemed very unlikely that Father Clarence's murder could be somehow bootstrapped into an Irish terrorism charge, Doyle fell silent for a moment, trying to discern another method to Acton's madness. "A UK murderer can still be sentenced to Maghaberry Prison, though—even if the crime's not committed in Ireland."

"Aye, but only the worst of the worst get sent to Maghaberry, missy. Terrorists, mainly."

"Right," she said again, and found that she was somewhat relieved by this dead end; whatever scheme Acton was weaving in his clouds of smoke, it seemed clear that it didn't involve sending Sir Stephen to Maghaberry Prison—thank God fastin'. Although she shouldn't feel relieved—not truly; Acton's vile cousin had indeed murdered a priest, and the fair Doyle shouldn't much care about saving the man from prison—instead, she should be hoping he suffered his just desserts, like any decent copper would.

There's something more here, she admitted to herself— something more than Acton's trying to arrange matters so that Sir Stephen sees the inside of a prison cell. And whatever it is, it is making me very uneasy. He's got a scheme in play—I can feel it in my bones—and there'd be no need for a scheme if he was simply trying to move a murder trial's venue to a more unforgiving place. Not that he could, of course—the murder wasn't an Irish one— and not that he'd truly want to, since it would also put his own mother at risk of going to prison. Therefore, in the end it seems fairly clear that there's nothing the poor man can do—his hands are tied, and Sir Stephen has managed to wriggle off the hook, because of it. But I know—as sure as the sun rises in the morning

—that none of this matters two pins; Acton's got some scheme in mind, and when that's the case, all the usual rules and procedures can be thrown out the window.

At this juncture, their escort brought them over to the Superintendent, and Doyle tried to decide how best to broach the subject she wished to broach, even though she wasn't sure what that subject was, to begin with. And it didn't help matters that the Pakistani man was in the midst of a discussion with the forensics team which did not appear to be going well; Doyle had participated in enough of these sorts of discussions to guess— gauging from their demeanors—that there wasn't a lot of evidence to be had. It was a shame, but it was usually the way of it, when the corpse was an old one; any useful evidence had long since washed away. Strange, that a likely-looking perp was hanging about when the decedent was discovered, but it may have been just a coincidence.

No, her instinct told her. Not a coincidence.

Surprised by this, she considered the ramifications with no small misgiving; it seemed that she was tasked with ferreting-out exactly who the strange man was, along with ferreting-out whatever scheme her wedded husband was masterminding with respect to his vile cousin and—and loosey-goosey Irish laws, apparently. Faith, it looked to be a busman's holiday, on all fronts.

With this in mind, she resolutely stepped over to hear about any leads that the team had discovered, but was suddenly brought up short, since the Superintendent had already indicated he was unlikely to share this sort of information with the likes of the Met's Doyle. And so instead, she lingered on the sidelines with an attitude of humble respect until the Superintendent noticed that she was waiting to speak to him.

"Officer Doyle," he said with a brisk nod. "Our sketch-artist is setting-up in the school."

"Right, sir," she replied, in her best helpful-witness voice. "I just wanted to mention that I hope my husband's not drivin' you mad; he's not used to not bein' the one in charge." This, to demonstrate that she was an avid protocol-follower, herself.

But her attempt to beguile the Superintendent did not seem to meet with much success, because the man was not about to engage in implied criticism of the illustrious Chief Inspector. "No, no; I cannot blame him for his concerns. A man must protect his family."

Doyle nodded her agreement, even though the danger to that selfsame family had been clearly exaggerated; after all, the last thing Sir Stephen would do would be to come after Acton's family —may as well sign his own death-warrant. Sir Stephen might be a fool, but even he was not that much a fool.

The Superintendent tilted his head in a discreet dismissal. "When you are ready, Officer Doyle."

"Yes, sir," Doyle replied, and had no choice but to retreat toward the school building, having discovered nothing remotely useful.

CHAPTER 6

*D*oyle sat at the hastily set-up table alongside the sketch-artist, as the young woman began to sketch out the outlines of the suspect's face. She'd brought along a "features" portfolio, which was intended to help the witness when it came to facial characteristics, but Doyle had decided that looking through it would only muddy the waters since she'd a fairly clear memory of what the man had looked like.

"He'd a long tattoo, all along the side of his face," she told the artist, indicating with a finger on the drawing. "He'd a shaved head, and so it was very apparent."

"What was the tattoo? Do you want to have a look at the 'known gangs' tattoo book?"

Doyle squinted, remembering. "No—it was nothin' familiar to me. And the tattoo itself seemed homemade—rather tribal, with windin' designs. It didn't seem gang-related—it was more a traditional Celtic design." Frowning, she made an attempt to sketch the design out with one of the pencils. "Somethin' like that."

"How far away was he?" O'Shaughnessy asked with a healthy dose of skepticism. He was watching the proceedings, and hovering over the two women in a rather annoying fashion.

"At least a hundred feet," Doyle admitted. "But he stood out, amongst the trees—stood out like a sore thumb; I'd a good look at him."

"Seems you're the only one," the Irishman joked.

"Faith, I wish I'd taken a snap," Doyle agreed. "It's hard to believe he's not all over CCTV."

The artist's pencil poised over the sketch. "Were his eyes close-set?"

"Wide-set, instead," Doyle replied. "Had a high brow—had a clearly-defined jaw, too."

"Like this?" The woman said, sketching out an outline.

"No—more broad, than juttin'." Doyle outlined with a finger, as she thought about it. "His face had a lot of broad planes."

The woman sketched a bit more, and as the image took shape, Doyle remarked, "You're so clever; I'd my portrait done, once, and I'm that impressed by anyone who can draw a likeness. I'm more on my son's level, drawin' stick-figures."

Doyle could sense the young woman's leap of emotion, as she paused to look up. "I believe it was Javid, who painted your portrait."

Readily, Doyle affirmed, "Aye, that. She's amazin'—truly gifted. We went to her weddin' not too long ago; she married Sir Vikili, who's a famous criminal solicitor in London."

"I understand—" here, the artist hesitated slightly. "I understand that you and Lord Acton patronize Isabel Munoz."

Doyle blinked in surprise. Munoz was a fellow detective who sold paintings on the side, and she'd managed to acquire a respectable following, largely due to a best-be-forgot Soho showing that had devolved into a firefight. "Oh—yes. D'you know Munoz, then?" On second thought, this wouldn't be all that surprising, since Munoz had married an Irish copper from this very Garda, and often came over to visit his family.

Her color rising, the woman replied, "No—I've never met her. I only mentioned it, because my style is similar to hers."

The penny dropped, and Doyle found herself smiling kindly. It was clear the young woman had gathered-up her courage to ask a favor, and Doyle thought—for what seemed like the thousandth time—about how strange life was, that she'd wind-up being someone that others would look to, to try and obtain an advantage. It was a far cry from those days when she and her mother made do with a soup bone from the butcher's, because it was the week that the rental was due.

Doyle offered, "Would you like me to have a look at your portfolio? I'd be happy to, although I'll warn you that I don't know much about art, and such. That's more Acton's bailiwick."

"Thank you, Lady Acton," the girl said, beaming with gratitude. "I'd truly appreciate it."

O'Shaughnessy chuckled. "I'll never get used to hearin' you called a 'lady'."

"Me, neither," Doyle admitted, and they all laughed.

Leaning over the artist's shoulder, O'Shaughnessy reviewed what she'd drawn thus far, and offered, "Hah—that looks a bit like your Tommy."

Doyle half-stood to take a better look, and then decided that perhaps he'd a point. Joking, she said to the artist, "My toddler's not a murderer, I promise; please don't mention it to the Superintendent."

They all laughed again, but Doyle felt a bit foolish, and decided that she should have followed the protocols like she was supposed to, and used the features-book; she knew better, after all —she'd seen many a witness who'd turned out to be mistaken in what they'd seen, no matter how adamant their testimony.

The session then came to a close, mainly because Acton had sent Adrian over to escort her back to the playground—a not-so-subtle reminder that he wasn't best pleased with having his wife held-over at the site.

"Wow," Adrian said, looking over the sketch. "*That's* the suspect? I'm surprised they let him wander around on the grounds."

"That was my first thought," Doyle agreed.

He frowned. "Does the tattoo look familiar?"

Doyle shook her head. "No—it's more of a design, I think; the gang-tattoos are usually very clear about what they represent."

"I don't recognize it," O'Shaughnessy agreed. "It looks Celtic, so mayhap it just took his fancy. A shame that I was facin' the other way, and didn't see him—I'd have gone over to ask a few questions."

Doyle frowned slightly, because—come to think of it—she should have probably raised an alarm upon seeing the strange man amongst the trees, too—or at least signaled to Acton. She hadn't thought him a threat, but she'd been wrong about such things before, and it had been foolish to take the chance. She'd been too nervous about her stupid speech, and let this be a lesson.

After thanking the artist, she then walked outside with Adrian, who was looking over to the crime-site with great interest, being as dead bodies weren't a-penny-to-a-pound for him. "Do they know anything, yet? Lord Acton said the victim seems to have been there a while."

"Aye, it does look like it, and leave it to us to stumble across a corpse when we're supposed to be on holiday."

He frowned slightly, as he watched the forensics team start to wind-up the caution tape. "Seems an odd place for a murder."

She nodded. "It may have been a body-dump; he was murdered elsewhere and buried in the grove, where no one would think to look."

But Adrian was skeptical. "A lot of kids, climbing around here. You'd think there would be better places to hide a body."

Much struck, she could only agree. "Now, there's a good point. Someone wanted to bury him hastily, mayhap—he wasn't very deep, because there are a lot of old roots in that area."

"Creepy," he declared.

"Very creepy," she agreed rather absently, because there was something here—something in what Adrian had just said—

"I hope it's not going to interfere with the rest of your holiday."

Recalled from her abstraction, she shook her head. "I doubt it; we've done all we can do, and the Superintendent who's in charge doesn't want the likes of Acton underfoot—he's already been ridin' the poor man about Sir Stephen."

But Adrian only raised his brows. "Is Sir Stephen coming to join us, too? I haven't heard."

There was a small pause. "Forget I said, then—I may be mixed-up." She glanced at him in a teasing fashion. "Although I wouldn't be a'tall surprised if Acton told you to bar the door, if he does show up. Has he?"

Adrian smiled in acknowledgment. "Not in so many words.

I've been told that Melinda's coming for a few days, but nothing about Sir Stephen."

"Melinda's comin' *here*?" Doyle asked in surprise.

"Yes—she's coming in with Ms. Davies tomorrow. I'm to bring both of them in from the airport."

Doyle considered the very-interesting fact that their security-man was apparently unaware that Sir Stephen was being hyped to the local Superintendent as a dire threat, and the also-very-interesting fact that Melinda—who had featured largely in the Father Clarence murder investigation—was coming over to Ireland to join them when there was little doubt that she wasn't inclined to do so. Doyle ventured, "Is our Callie comin' along, too?"

Adrian grimaced. "No; I don't think she's too keen on a family holiday."

With some sympathy, Doyle offered, "Can't blame her, I suppose."

"No."

They referred to Acton's younger half-sister, Callie. The young woman hailed from Trestles—as did Adrian—and indeed, the two had been childhood friends, with Adrian carrying something of a torch for Callie. But as she was now dating a police officer in London, he'd been firmly relegated to the role of mere friend.

Callie had learned she was Acton's half-sister only recently, with Melinda—their old neighbor—having been revealed as Callie's birth-mother through a series of rather shocking events. Acton's awful father—long dead, now—had forced himself upon Melinda, back when she and Acton were sweethearts, and the resulting child had been adopted by a couple near the estate, with everything hushed-up.

But now that the secret had been revealed, Melinda longed to smother the girl with long-suppressed maternal love whilst Callie was firmly holding Melinda at arm's-length, and having a harder time adjusting to this new reality. Faith, so was Acton, for that matter; Callie tended to be something of a wild-card, and Acton wasn't looking to deal with any more wild-cards, having already married one.

So; Doyle's suspicion that Sir Stephen was only being hyped as a straw-jack seemed to be accurate—especially given her sure suspicion that Acton kept close tabs on his cousin, and was well-able to counter any perceived threats long before they happened. On the other hand, having Melinda come to town was a wrinkle, and Doyle was having a hard time understanding why her husband had brought the woman here. Acton wasn't exactly fond of having Melinda underfoot—she tended to be a bit wearing.

Doyle and Adrian emerged around the building to see that Acton and Miss Cherry were already herding the boys toward the van, and—upon sighting his wife—Acton walked over to meet her. "How went your session?"

"It went well enough—although the sketch-artist knows we patronize Munoz, and was angling to be added to our list."

With gentle remonstrance, he drew her to him, and lowered his head to hers. "For your own peace, you must resist these attempts, Kathleen."

She sighed. "I know, I know—you've already explained all this to me, husband, but it's hard for me to deliver a snub—I haven't got half your experience. And I felt a bit sympathetic, I suppose— she had to take her courage in both hands so as to seize the chance."

"Forward any correspondence she sends, and I will handle it."

"Don't snub her too hard," Doyle pleaded

"I will see if she deserves it," he said mildly. "Any trace on your suspect?"

"No—and I don't see how he could have just disappeared into thin air—no question he was standin' there, big as life. If nothin' else, he should be a 'known,' just based on his description alone." She thought about it. "He seemed mighty amused by it all."

"Not a good sign," he noted.

"Oh—no, I meant that he was amused when I was speakin'; I didn't see his reaction when we unearthed the body."

He frowned slightly, as they approached the car. "And they've no leads?"

"Not a pig's whisper, my friend; they probably think I made the whole thing up."

He glanced at her. "It is possible that the man you saw was unrelated—perhaps a vagrant? This looks to be an old murder."

"Aye, that thought's occurred to me, too—those bones have been restin' undisturbed for a good long while. The perp didn't look to be a vagrant, though—seemed fairly hale and hearty. Mayhap he's just good at evadin' the CCTV cameras—which doesn't speak well of his intentions, I suppose, especially at a primary school."

"Indeed. I wish I'd caught a glimpse."

She frowned. "That's what O'Shaughnessy said, too—I saw him, but I was too worried about my stupid speech to be distracted."

"It was a very good speech," Acton said sincerely.

She smiled. "Aye—I was that surprised, myself. Which reminds me, I've another little speech in mind, so if you've no plans for nap-time, mayhap we can go out on a walkabout."

This was not an innocuous request; as he well-knew, Doyle was not much in the way of a hardy walker-about, and so instead it meant that she wanted to embark on a discussion with no fears of being overheard. For his own part, Acton famously avoided discussions, and—to be fair—small blame to him.

But her husband readily replied, "Certainly," and she was left with the puzzling conviction that her request for a private heart-to-heart hadn't made him uneasy in the slightest.

CHAPTER 7

*A*fter they'd lunched and put the boys down, Doyle and her husband headed out the lobby of their hotel—a posh, elegant Georgian townhouse, which was just the type of establishment that Acton tended to favor; he was all about discretion and not making a splash. And neither was she, of course—it was half the reason they were so compatible; they were each fiercely private, although they'd different reasons for it.

Which also meant it was never easy to embark on a marital clearing-of-the-air—not for either one of them—but it was a necessary chore that Doyle took-up on occasion, mainly to let her husband known that he wasn't going to catch her sleeping. As he was well-aware, her intuitive abilities meant that she could usually tell when someone was lying—a talent that was very useful, when dealing with a husband whose actions weren't always above-board.

As they started down the pavement, she began without

preamble, "Why are we in Dublin, Michael? No one likes you, here."

"A historical prejudice, certainly. It is unfortunate."

"But you're pilin' it on, and makin' a general nuisance of yourself. Faith, I feel like I've gone through the lookin' glass; who are you, and what have you done with my butter-won't-melt-in-his-mouth husband?"

"I will apologize to the Superintendent," he reassured her. "I am sorry, Kathleen."

"But why are we in Dublin?" she asked again. It had not gone unnoticed that he hadn't answered the first time, wretched man.

He glanced at her with a trace of confusion. "We are here to dedicate the science-lab."

But she shook her head. "No, we're not—or at least, that's not the true reason. Tell me what you're up to, husband." Subtlety may have been Acton's strong suit, but it wasn't Doyle's.

He walked a few steps, and then offered, "I am only concerned that Sir Stephen is under a great deal of pressure, and so I thought to remove our household from London for a time."

This was true, but she was well-versed in Acton's offering a partial-truth so as to throw dust in her eyes, and so she persisted, "I'll give you that you know him better than I do, but it seems to me that first and foremost he's a weaselly coward. Your bein' all up-in-arms doesn't make much sense to me."

Rather gravely, he explained, "I think he became alarmed when Melinda backed out of her interview, and stopped cooperating with Lady Madeline's investigation."

She was silent for a few steps, because this was a plausible concern—or at least, a plausible concern for Sir Stephen. The investigators were as yet unaware that Melinda had overheard the plotters—Sir Stephen and the Dowager—and then concocted her own counter-plot to marry the priest in secret so as to steal his fortune for herself. It was suspicious enough, that the priest left his family fortune to a sketchy foundation upon his unexpected death, but it was doubly-suspicious that the fortune had been hijacked by a secret wife, in the meantime.

But because she'd behaved badly, herself, Doyle had presumed that Melinda would disclaim any knowledge of the murder-plot when the investigators came to call, and keep her lip buttoned. But to everyone's surprise, she'd backed-out of her interview at the last minute, leaving the investigators with the sure sense that she had pertinent information she was unwilling to disclose.

Acton continued, "It is an ominous turn of events, and I am concerned that Sir Stephen may become desperate."

Doyle lifted her brows. "D'you *truly* think Sir Stephen might try to kill Melinda? Is that why you've whisked her over here, and you're jawbonin' at the Superintendent?"

"I'd prefer to err on the side of caution."

But Doyle was frowning, because she'd the feeling he was carefully choosing his words—a situation that always made her antenna quiver, because it meant he was being careful to sidestep any and all untruths. "But why wouldn't Melinda just lie to them, Michael? Unlikely that she's goin' to confess to her own role, in this mess."

"Melinda is unpredictable, unfortunately. As Sir Stephen well knows."

Doyle blew out a frustrated breath. "Aye—no arguin' with that, I suppose. And it definitely doesn't look good, that she decanted."

There was a small pause. "I believe you mean 'recanted'," he offered.

"Thank you—recanted." Doyle looked up at him to smile her

gratitude, because Acton didn't like to correct her, even though oftentimes she'd use the wrong word in a sentence. But she'd begged him to please make the effort after a truly embarrassing gaffe in front of the Detective Commissioner, and so he'd promised that he would.

He continued, "It is a volatile situation, and I'd feel better if Melinda stayed here in Dublin, for the time being."

This all rang true, and it also explained why Acton hadn't been keeping his wedded wife informed of these events—he didn't want her to know that he was truly worried about what his wretched cousin might do. Sir Stephen may be a cowardly weasel, but he was a cornered cowardly weasel, and therefore presumably dangerous.

Nodding, she slipped her hand into the crook of his elbow in a show of sympathy. "And isn't it ironic, that you're in the one place where the local authorities aren't much swayed by your illustrious heritage? Not to mention that this Superintendent's somethin' of a jobsworth, which must be a crackin' annoyance to a sword-swinger like yourself."

"On the contrary, he is only following protocol and I cannot fault him for it."

She smiled, because—rather surprisingly—this was true. "Faith, who *are* you? You marry a man, and you think you know 'im."

With an answering smile, he covered her hand with his own. "I am not saying that I necessarily agree with his approach, but I can understand it."

"Well, speakin' of things I can't understand, why have you taken-up smokin', again?"

They walked a few paces in silence, and then he said quietly, "I am sorry, Kathleen."

She squeezed his arm in sympathy. "Fah—nothin' to be sorry for, but it's not a healthy habit, Michael."

"A slight relapse, is all. I will stop, my promise."

She glanced up at him. "*Can* you stop? Mayhap you need one of those patches, like Savoie used."

"If I must, I will use one."

"Good—I don't have fond memories of seein' you smokin'."

This was true; the only other time he'd had a relapse—that she was aware of, anyways—was when he'd been weaving a plan to take-down a reporter who was about to expose his questionable enterprises. And the clouds of smoke were fitting, in a way, because the plan had been complicated and foolproof—mainly because he'd known exactly how the woman would react to unforeseen events.

Doyle's scalp prickled, and she was suddenly filled with misgiving; Acton was smoking—smoking and telling her that Sir Stephen might—predictably—do something rash. It was all a bit unsettling, in that it seemed to be a similar situation to what had happened with the reporter, when Acton had set-up his smoky scheme and then sat back to watch it all unfold. He was *conplated* —or whatever the word was—and in a strange way, it was almost more alarming than when he was in the throes of one of his black moods; at least when he was in a black mood, she knew what she was dealing with. Not that he'd been in a black mood for a long time, of course; he'd been making a huge effort to stay on his wedded wife's good side, and—fingers crossed—hopefully those rather frightening episodes were a thing of the past.

After weighing her options, Doyle decided to cut to the nub. "Tell me, husband, that you didn't drag us to Dublin so as to collar Sir Stephen, and make him pay for his misdeeds."

"I did not drag you to Dublin to collar Sir Stephen," he replied readily.

And there you have it, she thought with a huge sense of relief; I must have had my wires crossed, in thinking he was smoking-up some scheme to take down his cousin. Although—once again—she wondered at her own sense of relief; Sir Stephen was a despicable murderer, and if there was ever a time that she should be applauding Acton's vigilante-ways, this would be it.

He continued, "I will meet with Ms. Davies tomorrow, for an update on how the investigation is progressing."

"With Melinda in tow."

He nodded. "Yes. Melinda should stay of UK jurisdiction, for the time being."

Doyle could see the wisdom in this. "Aside from keepin' her close, you're also keepin' her out of subpoena-power, now that the investigators smell blood in the water."

"No criminal case has yet been filed," he reminded her. "But one may be soon, and so I am merely being cautious."

Doyle nodded, because if a criminal case was filed, it would mean that Melinda could be forced to testify by legal compulsion. And if she indeed told the truth, then Sir Stephen and the Dowager could very well face prison.

But—thinking about this—Doyle was faced with the one thing that didn't make a lot of sense, no matter how cautious Acton claimed he was being. "I'm just not seein' it, Michael; Melinda doesn't dare tell the truth, else it will be clear that she didn't step-in to stop the priest's murder."

"Failure to prevent a crime is not a criminal act, Kathleen."

She blew out a breath. "Right—although sometimes it seems that it should be. But I still don't think she'd tell the truth because she wouldn't cover herself in glory, if it all came out."

He nodded. "I would agree. But I thought it best to avoid the possibility of getting caught by surprise and so I will sound her out, while we are all here."

She squeezed his arm. "And you didn't want to tell me about any of this beforehand, bein' as Melinda's not the easiest person to have underfoot."

"She won't be underfoot," he was quick to assure her. "She will stay at a separate hotel."

But Doyle only replied, "Whist, Michael; no worries—I can't just ignore her, if she's here in town. Anyways, she's more likely to avoid us, since she's not one to tolerate little children."

He smiled. "A fair point."

"And speakin' of such, how long will your meetin' with Davies go, tomorrow? Shall I take the boyos and sally forth without you? I am bound and determined to feed the ducks."

"I doubt it will go all morning, but go where you will, and I can always catch up to you."

No need to ask how he would do it—Acton was a wizard at such things, and felt no compulsion to comply with the protocols that prohibited an officer from using police surveillance equipment for personal reasons. Which—come to think of it— rather made his behavior with the Superintendent even stranger still; she'd bet her teeth that Acton knew exactly where Sir Stephen was at any given time, especially if he was truly concerned about what the man might do.

Nothing is adding up, she admitted to herself, as she walked along with her husband. Although I definitely don't have the sense that he's over-worried about anything—which may or may not be a cause for alarm.

He bent his head to hers. "Shall we make another attempt to take the boys to listen to an Irish band, tonight?"

She laughed. "You'll never learn your lesson, my friend."

CHAPTER 8

hat night, Doyle had one of her dreams.

She had them on occasion; strange, vivid dreams that usually featured a person who was no longer alive—ghost dreams, which weren't very disturbing in and of themselves, save that the purpose of these dreams was always to send a message to her—and usually in the form of a warning.

These dreams used to bother her greatly, but Doyle had long ago become reconciled, since there'd been many an occasion when the ghost-message had, in fact, saved the day and prevented a coming catastrophe. Unfortunately, the message was never very clear—as though normal communication was a bit too primitive. Therefore, she always had to struggle a bit to discover what she was needed to do, and what was being warned against.

Sometimes the ghost was someone she'd known in life, and sometimes it was a stranger. On this occasion, however, it was a bit of both.

"Oh," Doyle said in surprise. As was the usual case, she was standing on a rocky outcropping, surrounded by darkness and with the sound of wind swirling about her, even though she couldn't feel it on her skin. Before her stood the strange man she'd seen in the orchard—muscular and ferocious-looking, even though—at present—he seemed to be regarding her with benign amusement.

"Oh," she repeated. "I didn't realize—sorry. I usually know when someone's—" tactfully, she avoided using the word "dead" and instead said, "—when someone's a ghost."

The man gabbled off something unintelligible.

"D'you speak English?" she ventured.

He frowned at her.

"Gaelic?" She asked in that language.

Again, he frowned, and raised his hands in the negative, which revealed that he'd crude tattoos, embedded on his palms.

"Usually, I've a translator in this situation," she ventured. She waited with a hopeful air for a beat or two—mayhap whichever ghost was supposed to translate for this fellow had got hung-up, somehow, and was running late. But she continued to be left alone with this fearsome individual, who—despite all appearances—didn't seem to be a bad sort. She'd sometimes been visited by evil ghosts—although it usually took her a while to catch on to this fact—but for some reason, she was fairly certain that this fellow didn't fall into that category.

"*Gersemi, dóttir,*" the man said with quiet emphasis, and used his hands in a pantomime, spreading his fingers wide as he indicated the ground below him. "*Blót-herloff.*"

Slowly, she shook her head. "Not a clue. Sorry."

He appeared to think about this for a moment, and then pantomimed a tree, his fingers spread as though they were branches. "*Holt. Hoddmímis-holt. Onshold-Yggdrasill.*"

"The trees," she guessed. "You were hidin' amongst the trees?"

He put his hands on his hip for a moment, regarding her thoughtfully, and then he bent to pantomime an unmistakable digging gesture.

Doyle's brow cleared. "The dead man? Did you bury the dead man?" She put a hand at her neck, and pantomimed a dead person who'd been hung.

Very pleased that she'd got something right, he nodded. "*Já.*"

"Are you the one who killed him?" she ventured with a tentative gesture at her own head, having a very good guess at the answer.

Again, he said, "*Já.*" He grinned, and when he did so, she could see that his incisors had been filed into points.

There was a small silence, whilst Doyle contemplated with some dismay the unrepentant murderer who stood before her. "You mustn't go about killin' people," she offered a bit lamely. Truly, it would helpful to have a bit of guidance, here—it seemed very unlikely that she was tasked with admonishing such a person, especially considering the language barrier.

In response, the man pantomimed tree branches again, his hands upheld over his head with his fingers spread. "*Yggdrasil. Holt. Hoddmímis-holt.*"

"Yes; are the trees important to you? I like them, too, and I'm sorry we had to dig-up so many of them, but the others will remain just as they are. We had to sacrifice them for the future of the school, you see; not everythin' can stay the way that it was, no matter how much we wish that it would."

"*Gersemi, dóttir,*" he repeated with a tinge of exasperation, and again made the digging gesture toward the ground.

Frowning, she decided that he was trying to offer an explanation for the murder, and ventured, "Who was he? You must have wanted him good and dead, what with the rope, and the spear though his head." Again, she indicated on her own forehead.

"*Blót*," he agreed, making an enthusiastic thrusting gesture as though he was holding a spear, and very pleased that she was getting the drift.

"Was it self-defense?" she ventured. The fact that the dead murderer was standing before her and trying to convince her of something seemed to indicate that she was needed to perform some task—perhaps exonerate him? This hadn't occurred to her—mainly because the perpetrator didn't look to be a "just cause" sort of murderer. But on the other hand, here he was in her dream, and trying to persuade her to do something— very sincere, he seemed, despite his ferocious appearance.

Doubtfully, she pointed out, "I'm not sure that I can swing a self-defense argument for you, if this fellow was killed two different ways. It would be quite a stretch."

Again, the man made the "trees" gesture. "*Yggdrasil. Onsholt— gersemí, dóttir.*"

Frowning, she stared at him in frustration, since they didn't seem to be moving forward in any respect. She explained, "I don't know as there'd be much point to pursuin' it, anyways. There's precious little evidence, and if you're already—" she caught herself, "—already a ghost, there's little to be done."

Suddenly struck, she ventured, "Unless you're not the true killer, and you want me to bring 'im to justice? Is that it?" She brought her hands to her breast, and then indicated the ghost before making a gesture indicating the body on the ground. "Was the dead man your kinsman, mayhap?"

The ghost grinned again, showing his horrifying teeth, and then pointed to her, before bringing his owns hands to his breast, and then making a bicep in the universal gesture indicating a man.

"*Acton*?" she asked in abject astonishment. "You think *Acton* had somethin' to do with this?"

He chuckled, amused, and she stared at him, completely bewildered. On second thought, however, this would actually be more in keeping, in that oftentimes the ghost-messenger would give her a head's up about an unknown Acton-scheme that was in dire need of stamping-out. But—try as she might—Doyle couldn't see it.

Shaking her head slightly, she offered, "I think you're barkin' up the wrong tree, my friend. Acton had no idea we'd a code-eighteen—no idea a'tall."

Her companion sighed, and put his hands on his hips. "*Gersemí, dóttir,*" he repeated, and then she was surprised to suddenly find herself awake, and staring at the hotel room ceiling.

CHAPTER 9

The following morning, Doyle was sitting at their suite's dining table after finishing-up breakfast with the boys. Acton had excused himself to make some phone calls from the spare room he'd set up as an office—he was never truly on holiday, being as he had to keep tabs on his caseload lest the villains in London take advantage of their own holiday from him.

Miss Cherry was not due to appear yet; as was his usual when they traveled, Acton had reserved the entire floor of the hotel, both for security purposes and to give the family some privacy, since the staff would each have their own rooms to retreat to in the evenings. This was to the good, in that Doyle didn't like to have a nanny at her beck and call twenty-four hours a day; it was too tempting to allow someone else to handle the day-to-day chores of motherhood, and it seemed a slippery slope.

Reynolds, however, always came-in early to prepare breakfast in that Acton drew the line at having to prepare a meal by himself. Idly, Doyle watched as the butler tidied up the suite's kitchen in his precise and efficient way; he very much enjoyed it on those rare occasions when they traveled, because it gave him the opportunity to field-marshal the staff at the hotel—something he enjoyed above all things.

Doyle had moved Edward and Tommy to the floor, where they were playing with building blocks after the breakfast-jam had been carefully washed off their hands—she'd learned a hard lesson, yesterday—and so Doyle finally had a few quiet moments to think over her dream, and the puzzle that was the dead murderer.

It was passing strange, that she didn't have a translator this time around, and so she'd no idea why he'd shown up; obviously, it had to do with his murder-victim—that couldn't be a coincidence. And it was doubly-strange that he seemed to want to finger her husband, even though she knew as a certainty that Acton had no connection a'tall to the dead man at the school— save for the fact it served as an excuse to needle the Superintendent some more. Which was another strange twist, that her normally-polite husband wasn't being polite with the man, even though he was politely letting Lady Madeline's investigators wreak havoc in their lives—faith, the world had gone topsy-turvy.

Could the benign ghost want Acton to exonerate him? That didn't make much sense, though; this wasn't Acton's case, and besides, it seemed to her that the ghost was cheerfully unrepentant—readily admitting that he was the one who'd killed the man, and showing not a shred of remorse. But his reference to Acton had given her pause, mainly because she'd the sure sense that the ghost knew something that the fair Doyle didn't know. It wouldn't surprise her if the ghost knew exactly why Acton was smoking again—smoking, and bound and determined to drag his entourage over to Dublin for some reason. And—lest we forget—content to sit back, and await events.

"Reynolds," she asked with a knit brow. "What's the word when you're happy to let things just go along as they are?"

The servant paused to consider this. "Content, madam?"

"No—I want to say 'conplated' but I don't think that's right."

"Complacent, madam?"

She lifted her brows. "Aye, that's it. Good one, Reynolds."

The servant advised, "There is also 'conciliatory', madam, which indicates a placative nature."

She gave him a look. "Now you're just showin' off."

"Rather an attempt to be helpful, madam," the servant replied, very much upon his dignity.

"Aye—and I do appreciate it, no matter how sleeveless the task. Poor Acton hates havin' to correct me, but I'll never learn, else."

"Exactly, madam. And I would hope my own suggestions are taken in the spirit they are intended."

"Whist; you're much-appreciated, my friend."

She watched as Reynolds laid down a plate of toast and jam for the boys on the floor—he was about to learn a hard lesson, poor man—and thought about Acton's strangely complacent attitude. There was something brewing, and she couldn't make heads nor tails—although, on reflection, it seemed a bit ominous that the ghost had made his laughing reference to Acton just after she'd asked him if the murder-victim was his own kinsman. It certainly seemed to indicate that her original suspicion—that Acton was going after Sir Stephen—had some merit, or at least, the ghost seemed to think so.

But Acton had decanted this theory—or whatever the right

word was—and he'd been telling the truth, when he'd said he wasn't going to collar his wretched cousin.

And yet meanwhile, they were all supposedly on high-Sir-Stephen-alert, which was another thing that made little sense. Doyle knew, as a certainty, that Acton could put a stop to Lady Madeline's investigation any time he wished; if nothing else, he could shovel a mighty sum of money the woman's way, since money had a way of smoothing-over any and all wrongs, especially if the amount offered was large enough. But Acton had chosen not to put this situation to bed, and so instead they were living with this female hornet buzzing about their heads.

I think that's what the argument in London was about, she mused; Sir Stephen wanted Acton to muscle-in and put a stop to the Father Clarence investigation, but Acton's not stopping anything for love or money. Which truly doesn't make a lot of sense—my husband definitely doesn't want the scandal, and that's miles more important to him than anything else, even more important than Sir Stephen's getting his just desserts. And meanwhile, she'd a benign murderer-ghost who was throwing up a caution about her wedded husband; a ghost that—presumably—she'd never have met, save that Acton had been bound-and-determined to visit Dublin for reasons unknown.

With a sense of resignation, she decided that she'd best quit shirking what seemed to be an obvious call-to-action, and asked, "Reynolds, what's the language where '*já*' means 'yes'?"

The servant paused. "That sounds a bit Scandinavian, madam."

"How about '*gersemí*,' does that ring a bell?"

"Perhaps a bit of context would be helpful, madam." This was his polite way of reminding the Lady of the House that she was sometimes mistaken, when it came to her choice of words.

Slowly, she shook her head. "I'm not sure what the context was —more's the pity. And there were some others words, too —*onsholt,* and—and *Yggdrasil.*"

The servant raised a brow, as though he was not quite certain he'd heard her aright. "Yggdrasil, madam?"

She looked up at him. "Aye—d'you know what it means?

"Yggdrasil refers to a sacred tree, madam. It is from Viking lore."

Doyle's stared at him as the penny dropped. "Ohhh—a *Viking,*" she breathed. "Now, there's somethin' that *finally* makes a bit o' sense."

"I beg your pardon?"

Doyle nodded thoughtfully. "The Vikings founded Dublin, y'know. Lived here for a long time, as a matter of fact—in school, we'd all take a field trip to the Woodstown excavation for senior year."

The servant nodded, clearly at sea but making a mighty effort to follow along. "Shall we take Master Edward and Master Tommy to visit the excavation, madam?"

"Holy Mother, Reynolds—bite your tongue. They're not museum-ready, and the curator would toss us out in a pig's whisper."

"As you say," he agreed, and decided to whisk the jam plate from the floor, having become alert to the perils of this misjudgment.

Thoughtfully, Doyle stared out the window. "And trees were important to the Vikings."

"Yes, madam; I believe their religious beliefs were largely animistic, and trees were seen as having cosmic significance, deriving from Odin's experiences with Yggdrasill."

Doyle discarded those portions of this explanation which were incomprehensible, and instead focused on what seemed to be relevant. "I don't think he's *angry*," she observed slowly. "Even though we cut down the trees. It's more like he's tryin' to explain somethin', and I'm not catchin' on."

"I am afraid I'm not following, madam."

"Neither am I," she admitted. "Thanks, Reynolds. D'you think you can write down the name ye—yderill—"

"Yggdrasil, madam."

"Yes—could you write it down? I may need to do some research."

The servant ably hid his surprise that his mistress would express such an intention, and dutifully wrote the word on a slip of paper.

CHAPTER 10

*a*cton emerged from the suite's spare room, and came over to kiss Doyle in greeting. Upon sighting his father, Tommy beamed from his position on the floor and held his hands aloft. "Paddycake!"

"That one's yours," Doyle noted, as she sipped her coffee.

Her husband dutifully lifted Tommy to hold him at arm's length, as he carried him to the sink. "Let's have a wash-up, first."

Armed with her new information, Doyle rose to accompany him. "Have you learned anythin' new about the St. Brigid's victim?"

"It is quite extraordinary," her husband replied, as tried to keep Tommy's rather slimy hands away from the sprayer nozzle. "The Coroner believes the remains may be nearly a thousand years old."

"Aye," she confirmed. "I think he was a Viking."

Acton raised his brows, as he set Tommy upright on the floor so as to rub him down with the dish towel. "It is possible, although there was no ornamentation on the corpse."

She lowered her voice. "I don't mean the victim—I mean the fellow I saw in the grove."

Acton paused to meet her eyes, and she felt a bit sorry for her husband; he was torn, because whilst he might feel—deep in his heart of hearts—that his wife was a bit mad, he had to acknowledge that oftentimes, her madness had proved very helpful.

She added, "I think he was worried about the school's uprooting the trees—it was a sacred grove, or somethin'."

Having got past his initial reaction, her husband now nodded thoughtfully. "Certainly, the corpse could have been from a ritualistic murder. That would explain the two different implementations."

"Paddycake," Tommy insisted with upheld hands, since his father seemed to have forgot.

Acton crouched down to participate in the slapping game as Doyle thoughtfully leaned against the kitchen counter and watched them. "Nasty bunch, the Vikings were; they'd human sacrifices, in their religious protocols—the nuns would compare them to the villains in the Old Testament."

"Yes," he agreed, as he patiently held still for Tommy's little hands. "They showed no quarter to their enemies."

"Rather like you, Michael," she teased. "I wouldn't be a'tall surprised if there was a Viking or two in the Acton family tree— your family motto should be 'Take No Prisoners'."

With a small smile, he observed, "The Normans were called the Normans for a reason, certainly."

"Now, there's a reference that flew well-over my head."

"And it's such a lovely head," he said, rising so as to bestow a kiss upon it. Over Tommy's protests he said, "That's enough for now."

Tommy retreated back to Edward and the building blocks as Doyle lifted her face to invite another, more lingering kiss. "Well, you're in a good mood, for someone who's got to sacrifice his mornin' to the likes of Ms. Davies."

It had not escaped Doyle's notice that her husband didn't much like the formidable solicitor; although it was very subtle, she was alive to the signs—Acton's tone got a bit clipped, whenever he interacted with the woman. But it spoke to the woman's talents that he'd nevertheless hired her to fend against the Father Clarence investigation, and small blame to him; Davies was ferocious and tough—just the sort of solicitor to make the opposition tread lightly.

Acton folded her in his arms, as they leaned back to keep watch on their sons—it was never a good idea to turn their backs for too long. "I'd much rather be feeding the ducks, believe me. But if a criminal case is indeed filed, we should be prepared."

Uneasy, Doyle lifted her face to his. "Could they force you to testify? Or me?" She'd a tendency to gabble, when she was nervous.

"Certainly, but we have no direct knowledge, and so I doubt it would get that far. We may be asked to file a statement under oath to that effect."

"Aye," she said thoughtfully. "Melinda's the only one with direct knowledge—aside from the culprits, of course. And it doesn't seem likely that she'd tell the truth, since she wouldn't want to expose her own role in this little holy-show." She made a face. "I'm torn, because—whilst I understand why it all has to be thoroughly swept under the rug—it's so crackin' unfair, that poor

Father Clarence was murdered and no one will be held accountable."

Philosophically, he offered, "Perhaps we can find some comfort in the fact that the plan to seize his family fortune did not succeed."

She blew out a breath. "Only because Melinda trumped their nasty plan with her own nasty one. That's cold comfort, husband."

Idly, he ran his hands down her arms, and then began playing with her fingers. "Then perhaps we might find comfort in Sir Stephen's current discomfort."

Aha, thought Doyle, suddenly alert; I think my husband is definitely finding comfort in Sir Stephen's discomfort—and mayhap that's why he's making no move to shut down this investigation. He's like a cat, who's toying with a nasty little mouse; it's a relatively small measure of punishment for what was done, but at least it's *something*.

Aloud, she said, "I suppose that's true; he's twistin' in the wind, and little did he know that a priest would have such a harridan for a mother—although you can hardly fault her, poor woman. It must be coals atop the fire, that her son was such a nodcock, and was fallin' for underhanded schemes left and right."

As he continued playing with her fingers, Acton agreed, "He did seem rather naïve, and ripe to be a victim."

"Aye, we see a lot of that, unfortunately."

This was only too true—many a homicide victim wound-up dead because they'd been far too trusting. Faith, the fair Doyle was rather naïve and trusting herself, save that—luckily—she'd a warning mechanism, and that selfsame warning mechanism was currently letting her know that—despite his words—her husband did not truly believe that a criminal case would ever be filed in Yorkshire, nor did he think there was the remotest chance that either one of them could wind-up on the witness stand.

Considering what was at stake, his attitude seemed far too—too complatent, or whatever the stupid word was. She'd seen him furious at his perceived enemies—Philippe Savoie serving as a recent example—and if anyone took the palm in making him furious, it was Sir Stephen. Yet here he was, discussing these cataclysmic events as though he didn't much care, one way or the other.

Whilst she tried to decide how to ask him something that might reveal whatever cards he was hiding up his sleeve, he advised her, "You've received an email from the sketch-artist."

She made a face. "You're such a *spy*, Michael; what if I had a secret boyfriend that I didn't want you to know about?"

Practically, he pointed out, "He wouldn't stay secret for very long."

She quirked her mouth. "Nor would his life expectancy."

"Very true. But I wanted to show you what she sent."

He rose to fetch his laptop, and—after opening-up her correspondence—turned it around on the counter so that she could see the screen.

"Wow," Doyle breathed in wonder, pulling the screen closer as she did so. The drawing that was presented was modern and a bit abstract, but there was no mistaking the subject. It was Adrian, only he was portrayed as an African tribal leader, wearing a feathered cape, and poised atop a lookout.

"That's *somethin'*," she declared in all admiration. "And she only saw him for a few minutes, Michael—he must have made quite the impression."

"Or she saw that you were fond of him, and sought to please."

"I suppose. She does look to be talented, though. And I have to admire her mettle, in shootin' for the moon."

He shut the laptop. "I will respond, if that is agreeable. I will wish to delve into her bona fides, first."

She smiled, and nestled into his embrace. "That sounds a bit saucy, Michael; especially when I recall how you delved into my bona fides, when first we met."

He lowered his head to hers and murmured," I could hardly sleep, for wanting to delve into your bona fides."

Laughing, she lifted her face to kiss him soundly. "You are indeed a romantic," she declared. "No matter what O'Shaughnessy thinks."

"What's this?"

She sighed. "He was speakin' out of school, which is his usual m.o.—the man has no filter. And you're a kind man, to tolerate him on my behalf—unlike the Superintendent, who is nowhere near as high on your 'tolerance' chart."

He made a sound of annoyance. "Unfortunately, with the news about the age of the bones, the Superintendent is now trying to decide whether he is obligated to contact Heritage Ireland."

"Oh-oh," said Doyle in alarm. "Don't tell him there's Vikings involved."

"There was no ornamentation on the body, which was fortunate."

Thoughtfully, Doyle rested her head against his chest. "Aye—the victim wasn't a Viking; instead he was the local chieftain, which was why he was the blood-sacrifice."

There was a small silence.

"Or so I'm led to believe," Doyle added lamely. Faith, she needed to watch her tongue; she was every bit as bad as O'Shaughnessy.

Smoothly, her husband continued, "I am trying to convince the Superintendent that the find is not worth calling a halt to the construction project, in that the Heritage organization tends to take its time."

She made a face. "Aye—when Father John found those old documents under the church floorboards, he didn't say a word about it, for fear the National Trust people would get involved."

"A very similar situation."

She sighed. "Good luck to you; the Superintendent's a stickler for the protocols. Not to mention he's probably inclined to run counter to anythin' you might suggest."

"I will confess it is an unfamiliar feeling."

She laughed, and twined her arms 'round his neck, which inspired another lingering kiss. "Aye—and good on him, not to be cowed to pieces like everyone else you meet."

He squeezed her fondly. "Save you."

"Oh, I'm cowed to pieces too, but I'm tasked with savin' you from yourself—I've got to stay sharp, in order to take-up my sword and buckler."

"You do admirable work."

Since this was said into her neck, she offered, "Shall I bundle you off the bed, husband? Ms. Davies can wait, whilst you delve into my bona fides."

Acton, of course, needed no further encouragement. "Let me alert Reynolds that we are not to be disturbed." He cast a meaningful glance over at the boys.

"You're goin' to get sticky, either way," she teased.

CHAPTER 11

*S*hortly after Acton had left for his meeting, Reynold announced, "The concierge reports that Mrs. Clarence has come to call, madam."

Doyle, who was in the midst of getting the boys ready for the ducks-outing, decided that this was a welcome development, since she'd have a chance to buttonhole Melinda without Acton's being present. "That's grand, Reynolds—tell them to send her up."

In a few minutes, Reynolds opened the door to greet the woman courteously. Melinda was a tall, willowy woman of forty years or so, and every inch the languid aristocrat. Back when she'd lived on the neighboring estate to Trestles, she and Acton had engaged in a youthful fling that had—unfortunately—set off the chain of events that had resulted in murder, arson, and—as they'd recently discovered—a secret baby who'd been the result of Acton's terrible father forcing himself upon Melinda. It was all deeply disturbing, and Doyle often wondered if Melinda's vague, detached manner was something in the way of a shield—a means of protecting herself from what must be a spate of horrific memories.

Not that Melinda was without her own faults, of course, what with her recent seduction of an RC priest serving as an excellent example. It was all very shocking to the strait-laced Doyle, who'd long-ago decided that those aristocrats who were within her personal acquaintanceship didn't exactly inspire admiration—there was a lot to be said for being poor and ordinary, all things considered.

"Hallo, Kathleen," Melinda said, raising the fingers on one hand with a negligent gesture. "I thought I'd check-in."

"Good to see you, Melinda," said Doyle, as she finished tying-up the last shoe. "How d'you find Ireland?"

"A very odd sort of place," the other woman pronounced. "And I can't say as I know anyone."

"You know me," Doyle pointed out.

"I don't think you count," Melinda observed thoughtfully. "It's all very strange."

Doyle rose to help Reynolds with the boys' jackets. "We're headed over to the river, if you'd like to come along."

"Oh," Melinda said doubtfully. "We are walking?"

"We are," Doyle said firmly. "The boys need to burn-off some energy. Are you in?"

"I am," the other woman replied with a show of stoicism. She lifted her mobile. "Let me text the security-fellow."

Doyle raised a brow as she gave Tommy's sleeve one last tug. "You've a security-fellow?"

"No, you have a security-fellow, but he's handling me for the time being." She paused in texting. "I only wish he would handle me—he's *yummy*."

"Don't you dare set your sights on Trenton," Doyle scolded, as she herded everyone out the door. "The boys love him."

"I need someone to spend my money with," the other woman complained. "Callie's giving me the *brutal* cold-shoulder."

Since Doyle could hardly blame Callie—Melinda was not someone who recognized boundaries, as could be ably demonstrated by her secret marriage to a priest—she ventured tactfully, "It may be helpful to give the lass a bit of space, Melinda. And she does have that new beau, takin' up her time."

"A very nice young man," Melinda declared, as she drifted down the hallway after Doyle, her fingertips trailing along the wainscoting. "Although I always feel that I've got to be on my best behavior around him."

Amused, Doyle threw over her shoulder, "Do you *have* a 'best behavior'?"

"Only when I've no choice," the other woman admitted. "But I'm trying to show Callie that I'm fit for company."

They met-up with Miss Cherry and Adrian by the lift, and after the usual fits-and-starts that occur when one is trying to maneuver little children out the door, they finally emerged into the morning sunshine, Doyle pushing Tommy's pushchair whilst Edward walked ahead importantly, chattering to Adrian.

Thoughtfully, Melinda observed, "Your security-fellow is yummy, too."

Rather than act the scold yet again—Melinda was unlikely to mend her ways, after all—Doyle decided to use this opportunity to do a bit of probing, now that she'd the other woman all to herself. Therefore, with a show of casualness she ventured, "I'm not one to like havin' a security-detail every blessed minute, but Acton's tryin' to convince the police here that we're all under dire threat. I can't see it, though; Sir Stephen's a straw-jack, as far as I can tell." She glanced at her companion. "You know him better than I do, though; should we be worried?"

"I'm not," Melinda pronounced. "*Such* a little man."

"Save that he's a murderer," Doyle reminded her.

"True." Melinda sighed dramatically. "It *is* rather a shame that he's skating."

Diplomatically, Doyle didn't point out that Melinda could have prevented the priest's murder, herself, and instead offered, "Aye—it is a shame. But I think Acton doesn't want the scandal, mainly because his mother might wind-up in the dock."

Melinda chuckled. "Can you *imagine*? It quite boggles the mind. Although it does seem to me that Acton's worried about the solicitor's catching on—he's the one who suggested that I stop cooperating with her."

"Oh," said Doyle, blinking in surprise. "I didn't realize."

Melinda nodded. "It's true; he called me the morning of my interview, and advised me to duck it." She smiled at the memory. "Poor Ms. Davies; she was so *very* unhappy with me."

Doyle considered this news, and decided that it only made sense; Melinda was a wild-card, and couldn't be trusted not to say something out-of-school—especially to the shrewd solicitor. He'd never mentioned this little tidbit to his wife, though, probably because the man's wife tended to think honesty was the best policy—such a quaint notion, and the very opposite of his own.

Melinda sighed. "He also suggested that I cut-down on my alcohol consumption—rather mortifying, to be honest."

Doyle raised her brows. "Faith, did he really?" Doyle had always surmised that Melinda drank a bit more than she should, but—since Doyle was Irish, born and bred—this didn't seem a major failing. It was interesting that Acton had given her the advice, though; the man must truly be worried about what

Melinda might say when she was in her cups. And—come to think of it—this was a much more plausible reason for bringing the woman here to Dublin than claiming that she was in any real danger from Sir Stephen; he wanted to keep her in-pocket, so to speak, and monitor what she said and who she said it to. After all, Melinda was the keeper of many a horrifying secret.

Fairly, the other woman admitted, "Alcohol does tend to cloud one's judgment. And I should do what he wants; he's shown no sign of putting an end to this *distasteful* episode, and so I should try to stay on his good side."

Thoughtfully, Doyle nodded. "Aye—he's not, and you'd think he wouldn't have even allowed it to get this far." She glanced over at Melinda and ventured, "I wondered if mayhap he wants everyone involved to suffer for their sins a bit, even as he doesn't dare let the matter to go to trial."

"Perhaps," the other agreed. "Although I don't think even Acton anticipated how dedicated my erstwhile mother-in-law would be to her cause—I should have just let the interview go forward, and told them I knew nothing about any of it. When I backed out, I think it only raised suspicions." She eyed Doyle. "Have you heard? Now they're threatening to bring a criminal case." She shuddered delicately. "In *Yorkshire*."

"Aye—Lady Madeline is hell-bent on vengeance, I think."

"*Such* a nasty woman—thinks I'm a schemer."

Fairly, Doyle noted, "Well, you are, rather."

Melinda raised a surprised brow. "Oh. I suppose I am; fancy that—it must run in the family."

Frowning, Doyle didn't quite follow. "You aren't related to Sir Stephen, are you?"

Melinda explained, "I wasn't referring to Sir Stephen—I was referring to Acton. I'm his aunt, or something."

Doyle stared at her for a moment, and then started to laugh. "Faith, I suppose that's true—or his stepmother, if Callie is his half-sister."

With a small smile, Melinda remarked, "I only hope he remembers me in the will."

With some exasperation, Doyle scolded, "I'd rather my husband not die anytime soon, Melinda."

"Oh; of course—sorry. I'll remember him in my will, then."

Oh-oh, thought Doyle, suddenly struck. Oh-oh—

"Which way, Lady Acton?" Adrian called back, because they'd come to an intersection.

"Oh—sorry; I wasn't payin' attention. Head left, and then we'll come to a bridge to cross."

Very much alarmed by the direction of her thoughts, Doyle pulled out her mobile and texted Acton, "Join us when u can."

He texted back, "Yes."

His instant reply made her twist her mouth, as she slipped the mobile back into her pocket. He wasn't enjoying his meeting much, but she'd a feeling he was going to enjoy theirs even less.

CHAPTER 12

*T*hey'd spent an active hour exploring the riverbank, with Edward only wetting the lower portion of his trousers in the process, which seemed a victory to Doyle since Tommy had fallen tail-over-teakettle into a plaza fountain only yesterday.

Acton arrived to join them—although she noted that he'd changed out of his formal clothes first, clever man—and he was now standing beside his wife as they watched Adrian demonstrate how to skip stones to an eager audience.

Doyle had been harboring some very disquieting thoughts, ever since her conversation with Melinda, and decided that the best strategy was to try to catch her husband by surprise— sometimes she'd catch a glimpse of his reaction, before he buttoned himself down. To this end, she began, "Tell me, husband, that you're not tryin' to get Melinda murdered."

He glanced at her in surprise. "I am not trying to get Melinda murdered."

This was the truth, and his dismayed reaction made her feel a bit ashamed. "Sorry," she apologized. "I panicked a bit, because she told me that you were the one who told her last-minute to back out of her interview with the wretched investigators. I wondered, for a moment, whether you were tryin' to pressure Sir Stephen into murderin' Melinda so that we'd have an entirely new murder with which to throw him in the nick."

With gentle remonstrance, he replied, "Surely you can see why I advised Melinda to back out, Kathleen?"

"Aye—I suppose it made sense," she admitted. "Especially if she's been drinkin' overmuch; the last needful thing is for Melinda start tellin' her tale—although she'd probably lie without a shred of shame."

"Yes—I would imagine. But I'm afraid I cannot take that chance—she is somewhat unreliable." He paused. "And it is not beyond the realm of possibility that she would disclose other matters that should be best left unsaid."

He was referring, of course, to the mayhem, rape and arson that had figured in Trestles' recent history, and she felt even more ashamed that she hadn't even considered this angle. Small wonder, that he wanted to ensure that Melinda never told her tale; small wonder, that he was urging the woman to stay sober at this particular juncture in their lives.

"Of course," she agreed, and then repeated, "I'm so sorry I leapt to such a conclusion, Michael. It was a shameful thought—especially knowin' that you've assigned Trenton to be her security."

He put a fond arm 'round her shoulders and pulled her to him. "It is only a precaution—mainly it serves to keep her contained. And in any event, it is unlikely that Sir Stephen would attempt to kill her—he is not an overt killer."

"Now, there's a good point." This was a police term, indicating a murderer who wasn't bold enough to take action his or herself, but instead would use indirect means to kill their victims—Father Clarence's poisoning serving as an excellent example. "Forget I said—I lost my bearings for a moment. Tell me about your meetin', instead."

He took a resigned breath. "It went largely as anticipated. Ms. Davies is fairly certain the investigators will file a criminal case, and soon. They are very interested in putting Melinda under oath so as to compel her testimony."

Doyle made a wry mouth. "Well, you can hardly blame them—they must know she's the weak link, the same as you do. And it's a crackin' shame that your Melinda-stonewall plan seems to have had the opposite effect."

There was the tiniest pause. "So, it would seem."

Well, thought Doyle, as her gaze rested on the stones-skipping participants; there's an equivocal answer if I've ever heard one. Could it be possible that Acton *wants* Melinda to testify under oath? Surely not; as he'd just pointed out, heaven only knew where it might lead, and what the woman might say.

Deciding to probe a bit, she offered, "On the other hand—whether she's under oath or not—I'd be that surprised if Melinda didn't lie like a dog on the butcher's stoop."

"I would rather not rely on her discretion, though."

"Aye, that," she replied absently, because she was flummoxed by the truth of this statement—she was getting mixed signals, and nothing made sense. Again, she wondered if perhaps he was toying with the villains in this tale, so that they weren't sure whether he'd actually step-in to save the day. Because *surely*, he was going to—she'd the sure sense that her husband was completely unruffled; he didn't think there'd ever be a trial, and he wasn't truly worried about any of this.

"And along those lines, I would like to invite Ms. Davies over for dinner tonight, if you've no objection."

Doyle blinked. "Oh—oh, none a'tall." This was unlooked-for, in that her husband was not one for inviting people over.

Sensing her surprise, he explained, "I would like to discuss strategy without appearing to do so."

The penny dropped, and Doyle nodded. He didn't want to make it look as though he was pulling the solicitor's strings, even though of course he was—a very careful man, was Acton, and very good at covering his tracks. "Reynolds will be happy; now he'll have an excuse to harry the hotel staff."

He leaned to kiss her temple. "I hope you don't mind."

Rallying herself, Doyle declared, "Not a'tall, husband. And we do owe the woman a huge debt of gratitude, after Nigel Howard's trial." She glanced at him. "Should we have the boys eat with Miss Cherry tonight?"

"I think we will include the children," he decided. "It may help to make it an early evening."

She smiled. "You think of *everythin'*, Michael."

But—behind her smile—Doyle was, in fact, mighty uneasy as she watched her husband walk forward to take a turn at skipping stones. He was quite good at it, which was rather surprising until you considered the fact that he'd been a lonely little boy who was more-or-less raised by wolves, and therefore had a lot of idle time. And she should keep this sad fact to mind, whenever she'd the uncharitable impulse to push him into the river.

Because she was having just such an impulse. He was up to something—she was certain of it, and it was that frustrating that she couldn't make heads-nor-tails of what he was about. He'd put the cat amongst the pigeons, with Melinda backing out of her interview, and she'd bet her teeth that it was not a strategic blunder—he was far too clever. If he was trying to punish his awful relatives so that they'd at least suffer some comeuppance, he seemed to be taking a huge chance; Lady Madeline's solicitors would be licking their chops in anticipation, and no one knew better than Acton that things can go sideways fast, once a trial starts.

Knitting her brow, she decided to pull together those pieces of information that seemed pertinent, like a good detective would. Acton wanted them all here in Dublin, and well-away from English jurisdiction—that was the starting point. Why was that? He was also needling the Superintendent for not giving them extra protection—as "international-important-people," or something, even though anyone who knew Sir Stephen knew it was very unlikely the man was truly a danger to them.

So; she'd no doubt that he was maneuvering things so as to achieve some goal, but on the other hand, she didn't have the sense that he was swinging his usual sword to achieve that goal. Instead, he was *complacent,* and content to allow matters to unfold.

She paused for a moment, but decided that she'd the word right, this time. He was complacent—and it had been completely true, when he'd said that he wasn't going to collar Sir Stephen— which was a bit strange, since she couldn't shake the feeling that Sir Stephen's comeuppance was at the heart of all these strange and unexpected events.

But even that theory didn't make a lot of sense; after all, her husband's hands were tied, since his mother was lurking as a co-conspirator. Nevertheless, Doyle had half-way convinced herself that he was arranging for Sir Stephen's one-way trip to Maghaberry Prison, somewhere in all this.

But apparently, he wasn't. And he wasn't setting-up Melinda as murder-bait, which was a huge relief—faith, the fair Doyle was a bit crazed to have leapt to such a conclusion; she needed to take hold of her ridiculous self. But her husband was definitely up to *something*, and it didn't help matters that she'd a ghost showing up in her dreams; a ghost who'd no qualms about human sacrifices and—lest we forget—who'd made an admiring reference to her wedded husband. It seemed too much a coincidence, and—taking a leaf from Acton's book—she didn't believe in coincidences, at least not when it came to him.

She needed to focus on two things, it seemed; she needed to figure-out what the ghost was trying to tell her, and she needed to try and discover why Acton had brought them all here to Dublin —there must be a good reason.

CHAPTER 13

*a*rmed with her new-found resolutions, Doyle turned over options in her mind, and decided—with a sense of resignation—that she'd no choice but to go to a library to do some research, since she didn't dare look-up what she wanted to look-up on her electronics, what with having a super-spy in residence.

Dredging up a memory, she moved next to Melinda—who wasn't trying to hide her extreme boredom—and offered in a bright tone, "You know, Melinda; Trinity College has a nice old library, with some famous book of 'kelps' or somethin' on display. Come with me to take a gander, tomorrow."

"Are the children coming?" Melinda asked with some misgiving.

"No—they're not library-ready. It would just be you and me and our handsome security-fellows."

"I'm in," she agreed readily. "Are they allowed to lunch with us?"

"Unfortunately not," Doyle explained. "They're supposed to be keepin' an eye on things, and not fraternizin'."

"Spoilsport," the other woman observed amiably. "All right; only give me an hour's warning."

Fresh from his toddler-attempts to skip stones, Tommy made his way up the river bank toward them, his gait similar to a sailor's. "Paddycake," he announced to Melinda, and held up his hands.

"I beg your pardon?" the other woman asked.

"It's a pat-a-cake game Miss Cherry taught him," Doyle explained, seizing this opportunity to keep Melinda busy for a quarter-hour. "Just hold up your palms and grit your teeth."

With Melinda thus occupied, Doyle walked over to her husband so as to raise her new-hatched library-plan in a casual manner. "I've asked Melinda to go with me to Trinity College tomorrow mornin'; they've that nice park, there, and we can have a walkabout. You can't come, being as I'm goin' to try to see what I can winkle out of her."

He nodded in agreement. "Very well. Reynolds has expressed an interest in taking the boys to St Patrick's Cathedral for the mid-morning service, and perhaps I will accompany him."

"Don't let them touch the holy-water fonts," she warned in alarm. "Remember what happened last time."

"It can't hurt, to douse them in holy-water," he teased.

"Well, just a word to the wise, since it's Miss Cherry's day off."

He gave her an amused glance. "Apparently, Mr. O'Shaughnessy has offered to take Miss Cherry on a tour of the city."

She stared at him in abject horror. "*No,*" she breathed.

With a smile, he ducked his head. "Indeed."

Annoyed, Doyle blew out a breath. "Faith, you'd think you'd

be more annoyed than I am, husband; you're the one who's put her together with Tim."

"Better to let nature take its course, I suppose."

Crossly, Doyle observed, "Well, that's mighty complacent of you—although I suppose we can't lock her up in the attic, like they did in that famous governess story."

He tilted his head, and reluctantly corrected, "I believe it was the first wife who was locked-up in the attic, and not the governess."

"What*ever*, Michael. The point remains that we keep losin' our staff to romance."

Fondly, he pulled her against his side and kissed her temple. "I believe you often tell me that love is uncontrollable."

After a moment's struggle with her temper, she admitted, "Aye, that I do. I'm a wretched dog in the wretched manger."

Tactfully, he suggested, "Perhaps that fable is not quite *apropos*."

Annoyed all over again, she retorted, "If you're goin' to keep correctin' me hand over fist, Michael, we're in for a long afternoon."

"Forgive me," he said, and kissed her again.

CHAPTER 14

here were entertaining Lisa Davies for dinner at the flat
—the formidable solicitor joining them *en famile*, as
Reynolds liked to say, and it was going relatively well, all things
considered. The boys were on their best behavior—although
Tommy was still too young to have a 'best behavior' in the first
place—and Acton was also on his best behavior, being all kindly
and such, which—come to think of it—was not exactly a good
sign.

Although he was hiding it well, Acton was not a fan of Ms.
Davies—she was not his type, of course; the renowned solicitor
was rather sharp-edged, as compared to his soft-edged wife.
Nevertheless, here they all were, making the best of it, with only
the children oblivious to the underlying awkwardness.

"Have you seen Sir Vikili, lately?" Acton asked in a polite tone.
"How is the Dumont matter progressing?"

Davies smiled easily, and lifted her wine glass to her lips

before answering. She'd insisted on having wine, which had seemed a bit odd to Doyle; Acton didn't drink wine—being as he viewed it as a poor substitute for scotch—and Doyle didn't drink alcohol at all. In fact, Doyle rather wondered if their guest had asked for a glass of wine as a show of defiance, since perhaps she wasn't happy about being seated with the children at table. Which led one to wonder if mayhap Ms. Davies was as little fond of Acton as he was of her.

It wasn't over-shocking, of course—oftentimes people who worked well together didn't like each other much—but still and all, Doyle couldn't help but have the sense that there was a subtle battle, underway.

The solicitor smiled her reply. "I dined with Vikili Tuesday last, as a matter of fact; I met him at the Temple Bar Club, along with Javid and Vadik."

"Vadik Gabriel?" Doyle asked with interest. "He's datin' Acton's sister, Callie. Was she there, too?"

"No, but Vadik spoke very warmly of her."

This was true, and Doyle resisted the urge to meet her husband's eyes—here was one instance, at least, where his matchmaking had paid off.

Acton asked, "Is the club tolerable? I've never been."

"Excellent menu; the atmosphere's bit dry, of course."

Interesting, thought Doyle, as she addressed her berry cup—Reynolds had done a good job of serving courses that weren't impossible for little children to manage. Davies had never answered his question about the Dumont matter—whatever that was—and it did seem as though there was a skirmish underway, with Acton insisting on using everyone's formal titles and Davies countering by dropping first names, willy-nilly.

Doyle also had the impression—well-honed by her adventure in marriage—that beneath his polite pose, Acton was listening very intently to the woman's responses to his inquiries. There's a method, to his idle conversation, she decided; although I doubt very much that Ms. Davies is going to drop any information she oughtn't—she's far too shrewd.

As the silence stretched out a bit, Doyle offered, "I wish I'd half the talent Javid has; I always marvel at people who are so creative—it's as though she operates in a different realm than the rest of us."

Davies smiled, and gestured toward the two children. "Nonsense, Kathleen; your creative talent is sitting right here with us at the table."

This was said with a touch of patronizing kindness, and Doyle hastily turned the comment into a joke before Acton could say something cutting. "Faith, if that's the case, I definitely suffer for my art."

Davies laughed, and Reynolds—who was quick to note that the Master of the House had gone ominously silent, took the opportunity to serve their main courses.

"It's *purple*," Edward breathed in wonder, as he openly inspected Ms. Davies' plate.

"Eggplant," the woman explained to the boy. "Thank you, Reynolds; it looks marvelous."

As for herself, Doyle could hardly imagine anything less appetizing, and so she offered, "Would you like some butter? Nothin' beats Irish butter, and I always overindulge when I'm here."

"I am vegan," their guest explained. "So, no butter for me, thanks."

"Oh—sorry," said Doyle, and then quickly shot Edward a motherly glance that stilled the question on his lips.

"Not at all—I try not to make a fuss about it. And speaking of vegans, Javid's expecting, did you know?"

"Is she?" Doyle exclaimed in delighted surprise. "Faith, that's wonderful."

"Pleased as punch, the both of them—she didn't have any children with the first husband; he was something of a rotter."

"So I am given to understand," said Acton, who'd shot the man dead.

"What's a 'rotter'?" Edward asked his mother in a stage whisper.

"Have some butter," Doyle offered, and placed a generous dollop on his green beans, which had heretofore been neglected.

"Sorry—I'm not used to underage company," Davies confessed with a small smile. "On to more innocuous topics."

"I'm headed over to the Old Library at Trinity College tomorrow," Doyle volunteered, mainly because it was a change of topic and also had the added bonus of making her sound a bit more worldly. "Have you been?"

"Never," the other woman answered, a bit dismissively. "I'm afraid I'm not one for sightseeing."

"Neither am I, usually," Doyle confessed. "But I thought I'd go take a gander— they've a famous old book, over at the library."

"Oh?" Davies asked, in the manner of someone who was trying very hard to appear genuinely interested.

"I believe Mrs. Clarence is also going," Acton offered.

This sparked a genuine interest, and the other woman raised her brows. "Melinda's going? I should go, too, and use the opportunity to castigate her."

"You're welcome to join us," Doyle offered, making a mighty effort not to sound as though this was the last needful thing.

Davies laughed lightly. "No—I'd only lose my temper."

"Mum loses her temper, sometimes," Edward decided to mention.

"It's the hair," Doyle said lightly, as Edward's father shot him a quelling look. "It has a lot to answer for."

"Nonsense," said Davies. "Your hair is lovely, Kathleen—a true daughter of Ireland."

This, said with another trace of patronizing kindness which prompted Doyle to hastily joke, "'Tis a mixed blessin', this heritage of mine."

Davies lifted her wine glass and said dryly, "Well, you can't be blamed; Melinda would try the patience of a saint."

"Mrs. Clarence is a long-time friend," Acton remarked in an even tone.

"Not that she doesn't have her moments," Doyle hurriedly offered.

"Paddycake," said Tommy, who didn't want to be left out.

They all laughed, and the tension was broken but Doyle suddenly realized that the conversation didn't seem to be making sense, and so she ventured, "But—isn't Melinda your client, Ms. Davies?"

The other woman lifted a corner of her mouth. "No—I have withdrawn from her representation. Sir Stephen is my only remaining client, in the matter."

Doyle blinked. "Oh, oh—right; I suppose their interests may not be the same."

"No—actually it is because she is not following advice of counsel," the other woman offered kindly, as though explaining something to a child.

Reynolds suddenly appeared with a teapot, even though they were still on the main course. "May I offer sencha tea, Ms. Davies?"

"Call me Lisa, please," she insisted. "And thank you, I will."

"My mum drinks coffee," Edward informed their guest.

"Far too much," Doyle agreed in an overly-hearty tone, being as Acton had gone silent again.

"I drink coffee in the mornings, just like your mum," their guest told the boy, and Doyle had the feeling she was aware that she'd overstepped. Very shrewd, was Ms. Davies—as could only be expected; a high-level solicitor like she was would be well-versed in reading the room, so to speak, and retrenching where retrenching was needful.

Nevertheless, it was all a bit uncomfortable, especially since Acton—rather famously—doted on his Irish bride, and Ms. Davies would presumably know that the fastest way to get into his black book was to direct subtle digs at his better half. Which led one to the surprising conclusion that the woman was not in the least bit intimidated by the great and mighty Lord Acton.

Although perhaps this was not so surprising, after all; Doyle had well-noted that a large part of an attorney's success hinged on the ability to present an intimidating front. If you'd a reputation as a tigress—like our Ms. Davies, here—the other side was more likely to tread the path of least resistance, with Sir Vikili also serving as an excellent example of this phenomenon. Sir Vikili's renown was such that many a rightful case was never filed, if the famous solicitor was known to represent a particular client. Doyle didn't think this was necessarily fair—mainly because the system favored the blacklegs who could afford such counsel—but it was a fact of life, nevertheless, and here was a prime example; our Ms. Davies, here, felt absolutely no qualms about tugging on Acton's tail. If Doyle were in her position, she'd have had more than a few qualms, being as she knew the man well.

"How wonderful, that you are supporting your old school, Kathleen."

Doyle willingly accepted this proffered olive branch. "'Tis the eighth wonder of the world; I half-expect the Mother Superior to scold me to stand-up straight, just like in the old days."

"And now you're her benefactor; it must be very gratifying— quite the turn-around."

Again, there was the slightest tinge of patronage in the remark, and Doyle quickly joked, "No one's more gratified than the teachers who managed to push me through."

Acton said nothing, and into the silence Davies signaled to Reynolds. "May I have another cup? This sencha is delicious."

"Certainly, Ms. Davies," said Reynolds, who was not about to side with the guest in the first-names skirmish.

The evening thankfully came to a close soon after—mainly because the boys were showing glimpses of the insanity that lurked just beneath the surface when they were ready for bed. The adults all managed to part amicably, even as Doyle duly noted that there hadn't been a whisper of strategizing during the meal, which was supposedly the whole point of this wretched dinner-party.

In this, however, she spoke too soon, since Acton did pause to have a low-voiced conversation with Davies at the door. As he did so, Doyle took the opportunity to say to Reynolds in an aside, "Thanks for drawin' her off; Acton had her over because he's tryin' to be civil, I think, and he's not very good at goin' about it."

In a prim tone, the servant replied, "I am not certain Ms. Davies appreciates such generosity, madam."

"Aye, although I think he was givin' as good as he got." She gave the servant a significant glance, as she herded the boys toward the bathtub. "The man might be due for a swallow o' scotch."

"Very good, madam," the servant replied, and they parted in perfect understanding.

CHAPTER 15

*a*cton made short work of his scotch, but Doyle had shrewdly gauged his mood and decided that further restorative action might be needful. Therefore, with the boys safely abed, she climbed onto his lap to nibble on his neck, with the unsurprising result that he decided they should make it an early night.

After a very satisfying bout of lovemaking, she was lying atop him, lengthwise, with her cheek against his chest as she gazed at the diffused light coming in through the lace curtains.

"We should have lace curtains," she decided. "They're very pretty."

"If you wish." His hands were moving idly on her back, but she could sense he was still a bit agitated by this latest misguided attempt at having a social life.

She added, "My mum always longed for lace curtains, but we hadn't the money."

She could feel his chest rise and fall beneath her. "I confess it pains me, when you speak of such things."

But she only smiled. "It shouldn't, Michael; you can't change the past, after all. And we were happy, despite everythin'. I was poor and happy, whilst you were rich and unhappy."

"Yes," he agreed, his fingers lightly tracing her back. "Very symmetrical."

"I think a lot of what drives you stems from that, Michael— you were miserable growin' up, and you couldn't do anythin' about it."

This was a bit daring, because not only did Acton avoid discussions, he doubly avoided any discussions about what made him tick.

And so, she wasn't much surprised when he turned the subject. "I am sorry Ms. Davies was rude to you."

"Whist, she wasn't *rude*, Michael; more like she's so used to joustin' that it just comes naturally to her. And to her credit, when she realized that you were glowerin', she made a mighty effort to mend her ways." She tapped her fingertips on his ribs. "It shouldn't bother you more than it bothers me, Michael."

But he wasn't having it, of course. "You are my wife. You should be afforded a full measure of respect."

She teased, "You make it sound as though I'm just a placeholder, or somethin'."

"In a way, you are. To disrespect you is to disrespect the heritage."

"I understand," she soothed, even though she didn't, but had learned long-ago that there was no arguing with him on this subject. "Amazin', that the heritage married me in the first place."

Contrite, he swept his palms across her back and squeezed her to him. "I meant no insult, Kathleen; forgive me."

She lifted her head for a moment to kiss his chest. "A'course, you didn't, and I wasn't criticisin'—not a'tall. It *is* amazin', and good on you for bringin' it about. We're good for each other; I build you up, and you build me up."

"Yes," he agreed in a monosyllable, because they were treading into 'discussion' territory, and he'd gone a bit wary.

She smiled as she settled her cheek on his chest again. "And anyways, your lot was needin' a boost of hearty peasant stock, so as to brace-up your bloodline. Otherwise you'd all wind up like Melinda, who's like a reed, blowin' in the wind."

"Yes. Although Melinda certainly has revealed hidden depths."

"Aye—and I'm that surprised that she can scheme with the best of them; only goes to show that appearances can be deceivin'." She smiled. "And speakin' of such, she was that happy, to play pat-a-cake with Tommy."

His hand paused. "She was?"

Since this was asked with a full measure of incredulity, Doyle chuckled. "Aye. And let this be a lesson that we should be miles more patient with the boyo—a lot of people long for the chance."

But he observed with some disapproval, "Melinda's been inadept with Callie, certainly."

"If I'd the first clue what that meant, I'd probably agree."

He squeezed her to him. "It means she's been a little heavy-handed."

"Aye; a lot of that goin' around."

He was silent, and so she continued, "Everyone needs to give it some time—the poor lass is buffered on all sides."

"Buffeted, perhaps," he corrected gently.

"Thank you—buffeted. Callie's the type who doesn't like bein' told what to do, Michael, and meanwhile everyone's tellin' her what to do."

"The heritage is hers, also," he insisted. "And it is important that her actions reflect this."

"She's a champ, at pat-a-cake," Doyle replied. "None better."

There was a silence, as his chest rose and fell beneath her. "I am asking too much, am I?"

"A bit, Michael—let her find her feet, for heaven's sake, before you burden the poor thing with legacies, and such."

"All right."

She nuzzled his chest in appreciation, and then they fell into a contented silence, as she idly pulled at the hair on his chest and continued to gaze out the dim outlines of the window. "What's the 'Dumont matter'? Davies avoided answerin' your question."

He was silent for a moment, and she knew he was deciding how to respond. "There is no Dumont matter. I am conducting an experiment."

She blinked in surprise, and then guessed, "You're goin' to see if she races off to Sir Vikili, to find out what you're talkin' about?"

"Something like that."

Doyle frowned. "You'd think she'd have to be discreet, as part of her job."

"So, you would think."

She made a wry mouth, as she continued to contemplate the curtains. "Fine; you're not goin' to tell me what you're up to, husband. Seems very odd that you've hired the likes of her even though you don't trust her, and you don't like her much."

"I don't like anyone much," he pointed out fairly

"Save me."

"Save you." He raised his head up to kiss the top of hers.

"And your two little legacy placeholders," she reminded him.

"Forgive me, I put it inelegantly."

"Fah; its only me, Michael—no need to be elegant in the first place." Thinking about this, she asked, "If Davies isn't representin' Melinda anymore, then who is?"

"Melinda does not have representation, at present."

She raised her brows. "Faith, that looks bad. Small wonder Lady Madeline's people smell blood in the water—it's never a good sign, when counsel withdraws."

"According to protocol, Davies has little choice in the matter; counsel's foremost duty is to the court. If an attorney has direct knowledge of potential perjury, then he or she must withdraw from representation."

But Doyle only made a skeptical sound. "Pull the other one, Michael; Sir Vikili always represents lyin' liars who are the blackest of blacklegs, and he *never* withdraws."

"I imagine he is careful never to have direct knowledge of potential perjury."

Blowing out an irritated breath, Doyle observed, "*Such* a flim-flam; not to mention that it fills his wretched coffers, too—his clients are always the wealthy villains who tend to get away with things, thanks to him. To my mind, it's akin to bein' an accessory-after-the-fact, if you don't step-in and try to right the wrongs that you know were done. The Church thinks so, anyways; it's a sin to sit idly by, when you have the ability to right the wrongs."

"It is a fine line," he agreed. "On the other hand, everyone is entitled to a defense."

"I'd never make a good defense counsel," she admitted. "It's always cut-and-dried, for me." She paused and then added, "For you, too."

"Yes," he agreed, in another wary monosyllable.

She kissed his chest again. "There's one thing we have in common, at least."

"We have a lot in common," he protested.

"No we don't, but thank God fastin' that somehow, it works."

"Yes." He wrapped his arms 'round her, and squeezed her fondly.

He was getting amorous again, but Doyle decided she'd press him a bit further, whilst he was in such an amiable mood. "So; if Lady Madeline manages to get a criminal case filed, one would think that Melinda will have no choice but to unbutton to a solicitor. Your mother, on the other hand, is not goin' to unbutton to anyone under any circumstances, even God himself."

"It is doubtful either one of them would tell the truth, in any event."

"Aye, I suppose that's the savin' grace—which is a sad state of affairs, when you think about it. But if Melinda decides to tell the truth, everyone's sunk."

"We will cross that bridge when we come to it."

Now, that's interesting, she thought, as she continued to gaze thoughtfully at the window; he doesn't think we are ever going to cross that bridge. It seems more and more as though his plan, all along, has been to let everyone twist in the wind a bit before he charges in like the cavalry, and puts everything to rights. Which would also explain why he's so unworried—he knows there's no danger that a scandal's going to erupt, but he's very much enjoying the fact that the villains are paying some small price for their sins, and no one can figure out why he's acting as he is.

But this theory also made her very uneasy—that he seemed so certain, and so complacent. In her view, a lot of things could go wrong; Lady Madeline was bound and determined to avenge her son's death, and—after all—the man had indeed been murdered.

Thinking to give him warning, she offered, "You know, Michael; people aren't always so very predictable—there's many a slip, 'twixt cup and lip."

"I may disagree; people do tend to be predictable. It is half the reason the CID manages to make any arrests."

This was indisputably true, of course; she hadn't been on the job as long as he had, but even she'd noted that people's actions—and motivations—tended to run in very predictable patterns.

Teasing, she offered, "I suppose you've a point. After all, you knew I'd marry you in a pig's whisper, so long as you asked politely, and made it sound as though it was just routine."

He chuckled, his chest moving very pleasurably beneath hers. "Yes. Or at least, I thought the odds were in my favor."

"Well done, you. This particular placeholder is very grateful that you managed to pull the wool."

He ran his hands over her hips, pressing her to him. "Speaking of placeholders—"

"I see how it is," she sighed in mock-resignation.

CHAPTER 16

*T*hat night, Doyle had another dream.

Once again, she was facing the Viking, who'd his hands on his hips and was regarding her with what seemed like amusement mixed with exasperation, rather at odds with his ferocious appearance.

"*Dóttir,*" he said with a hint of impatience. "*Gersemí—onsholt.*"

Slowly, she shook her head. "I'm that sorry; we're in dire need of a translator."

Once again, he pantomimed stabbing someone with his spear, and then digging.

"We're not supposed to sacrifice people, any more," she decided to inform him. "It's a brutal way to go about things, and shame on you."

The ghost grinned, showing his fearsome teeth, and made his bicep gesture.

"Well, yes—Acton would make no bones about sacrificin' his enemies, and think it blood well-spilt. You and Acton have miles more in common than me and Acton, so shame on the both of you."

She thought about this for a moment, and then corrected. "He is tryin' to be better, though. He'd nothing to live for, before, but now he's decided that he'd rather stick it out with me and the boyos. So I think he's a bit more careful than he used to be about how things might play out. He used to be all fiery-lakes-of-lava, but now he's more like Sir Vikili, and at least makin' a pretense that he's tryin' to follow the rules."

Her companion held up his tattooed palms, indicating that he didn't understand.

"No, you wouldn't understand—it's not somethin' you could ken; your lot lived for your legacy, and thought that the best and greatest thing was to die in battle, so as to get written-up in the sagas. But then you'd miss out on the ordinary things that go along with livin' an ordinary life—which are pretty nice, even though they don't speak of such things in the history-books. I think Acton's learnin' that, finally—although it was a close-run thing, for a while. I've managed to temper him down a bit, which was no easy task, believe you me."

He shifted his weight to lean on his spear, and watch her with a bemused expression.

Slowly, she shook her head. "I wish I'd the first idea why you've shown up, and it all seems a bit pointless, if we can't communicate. So, I'm goin' to the library tomorrow to try to make some headway—hopefully I can get the gist. I've precious little, so far—all I know is you killed the victim as a sacrifice—all those years ago—and now we've dug him up, and we've dug up your precious trees, and you're none too happy."

With all sincerity, she spread her own palms in a gesture very similar to his. "I'm that sorry for it, but time marches on. We can't leave everythin' just the same as it's always been, no matter how much we'd like to. Old ways have to make way for new ways, which is just as it should be, I suppose. You can't hope to bind the future, after all."

With a sound of impatience, the Viking again made the "tree" gesture, raising his arms and spreading his fingers.

"Yes—I'm truly sorry, and I hate to be the one to have to tell you, but your poor trees have a bit more bad luck, comin' their way. The Superintendent is lookin' to let the historical people excavate the site, which will muck-up the school's construction plans and put everythin' on hold." In all annoyance, she groused, "There'll be a bunch of self-important bureaucrats trompin' about, thinkin' they have the ability to freeze history, when history's like a fast-movin' river that pays no mind to the likes of them."

Warming to this theme, she accused, "At heart, you're all the same—you with your sagas, and the bureaucrats tryin' to pick-and-choose what they think is important to remember, and even Acton, with his placeholder-heritage nonsense. You're all tryin' to stake your claim to history, but you're all whistlin' in the wind— history doesn't give two pins. And it seems so—so *desperate*, that you want to be remembered as 'important' to other people, when that's the wrong way to go about it. There's only one Opinion that truly matters, and heaven's the only legacy that's truly eternal; here on earth, everyone moves on—history moves on, and there's no point in tryin' to claim it for yourself just so you can feel that you mattered to people who've long forgot about you."

He stared at her blankly, and with some exasperation she continued, "Faith, it's much the same as I said in my speech at the school; you've no idea what's goin' to be important a hundred years from now—let alone a thousand—so there's no point in trying to frame-it-up to serve your ego, when you'll be long-dead anyways. Let the future sort the future—it seems so selfish and silly, to insist that they honor you."

Impatiently, the ghost repeated with heavy emphasis, "*Herloff, dóttir.*"

She sighed. "Aye; I'm gettin' you translated tomorrow, don't you worry."

CHAPTER 17

It was the following morning, and Doyle was walking across Library Square at Trinity College with Melinda —progress necessarily slow because Melinda was even less of a walker-about than Doyle.

It was a fair morning, and Doyle looked about her with interest; Trinity College was not a place she'd been familiar with, growing up, but she'd visited the last time they'd been here on holiday—even though it hadn't been much of a holiday. Their last visit had been marred by Acton's having to move heaven and earth to cover-up a nasty murder, and thus help a friend out of a very dicey situation. Which—when you thought about it—was basically what had happened with the Father Clarence murder, although that one involved his miserable relatives instead of a good friend.

But in the end, it didn't make much difference; in both cases, there were extenuating circumstances that required a murder to be well-and-thoroughly swept under the rug, and it was a shame, but there was no bunking it.

Indeed, the Dublin murder had been the first time that Doyle was forced to acknowledge that there may be times when her wayward husband had the right of it, and the justice system's protocols might have to be sidestepped for the greater good. Not that she'd been happy about it, but that little episode had brought home the fact that she'd been a bit naïve, to think that everything could be deemed right-or-wrong and black-or-white. Oftentimes, there were many, many shades of grey in-between.

And speaking of shades of grey, Doyle decided she may as well make an attempt to winkle information from Melinda, since that was the excuse she'd given Acton for this library-project. To this end, she mentioned in a casual tone, "We'd your ex-solicitor over for dinner, last night."

"You never have *me* over for dinner," Melinda complained.

Doyle smiled. "We never have *anyone* over for dinner, Melinda, and last night was a reminder of why this is. She and Acton locked horns, a bit."

Melinda shuddered delicately. "Horrid woman—so very *brash*."

"She'd good at what she does, I suppose—so there's that. You have to remember that's why you hired her in the first place."

But Melinda demurred, "It was Acton who hired her, not me. And it's a shame that he thought I should sacrifice alcohol at the same time—hardly fair."

"I suppose he wanted to make sure you'd your wits about you, and small blame to him." This, said with a great deal of meaning.

Melinda nodded in rueful acknowledgement. "Yes—I suppose his intentions are good. And Callie will be impressed if I make the effort—he pointed that out, too."

"Did he? Good on him, then." But Doyle knit her brow, because this attempt to straighten-out the Melinda-Callie tangle-patch did not seem to be in keeping with her husband's general attitude; it would be miles more likely that he hoped he'd never have to deal with either one of them, ever again.

Thinking on the strangeness of this, she glanced over at her companion. "Funny, that you're lettin' Acton pull your strings, Melinda."

"It is, isn't it? Although he did it so well, back in the day."

Doyle made a wry mouth. "No sex-talk about my husband, if you please."

"Oh—right; sorry."

But Doyle wasn't paying attention, because she'd had another thought; not only was her husband acting very much out-of-character in giving Melinda life-advice, but one might say that the advice was backfiring. After all, he'd urged Melinda to back out of her interview, which only made Davies withdraw from representation so as to make the investigators champ at the bit, and scurry over to speak to the Yorkshire prosecutors. Faith, if she didn't know better, she'd think that Acton was pulling Davies' strings, as well as Melinda's.

Confronted with these troubling thoughts, she mused aloud, "It's not as though he'd want to *undermine* her—Davies is top o' the trees. She was very helpful in Nigel Howard's murder trial, and you could see that Sir Vikili trusts her—and Gabriel does, too. Faith, they're all havin' dinners together, thick as thieves."

"More handsome men," Melinda sighed. "I envy you—you've *so many* in your orbit."

Doyle made a wry mouth. "I'd just as soon keep my eyes on my husband, Melinda."

Melinda chuckled. "We are definitely cut from a different cloth, then; I always used my husbands as a stepping-stone to seek-out the next one—although if I'd started with Acton, perhaps I wouldn't have felt the need."

Doyle decided it was hopeless, and changed the subject. "Sir Vikili is related to Callie's new beau, somehow. Did you know?"

"I did. And isn't he related to Acton's Assistant, too?" She furrowed her brow. "Nancy?"

"It's Nazy, and they're not related—she's Pakistani. As a matter of fact, we first met Nazy last time we were here in Dublin; she was thinkin' of becomin' a copper, and was an intern at the local Garda."

"Fancy that," said Melinda, in a tone of complete disinterest.

Doyle decided to enlarge on the subject, since it was much more interesting than her companion imagined it to be. "Nazy was very helpful in a murder case, here—a priest from London had got himself a knife through the eye."

"Really?" Melinda stared at her for a moment, and then made a sound of distaste. "How *extraordinary*."

Doyle reminded herself that she'd best button her lip instead of try to impress Melinda with all the gory details—that case had never been officially solved and with good reason, since it had turned out that the priest's death was a ritualistic vengeance-murder that was slated to go unsolved.

Doyle's scalp prickled, and she paused in surprise before realizing why it did; the corpse at the school had also been the victim of a ritualistic vengeance-murder, poor fellow, but then again, if you went at the Vikings you had to be prepared to pay the price.

Her scalp prickled yet again, but before she could figure out why this was, Melinda's plaintive voice cut into her thoughts. "I wish Callie was here; she hasn't *any* time for me—wouldn't make the trip, no matter how much I pleaded and begged."

"Faith, Melinda—give the lass some time to adjust, it's all been quite the shock."

With a sigh, Melinda replied, "That's what Acton says, too. And I suppose it doesn't help matters, that I've a murder investigation hanging over my head."

"It's a disadvantage," Doyle agreed dryly. "Chin up, things will get better."

But Doyle offered the words in a perfunctory fashion, because they were coming up to the Library steps, and it was time to detach from Melinda. In a casual tone, she announced, "Oh—here we are; I wanted to go into the historic-archives section to see if they've any old photos of St. Brigid's School—I'm goin' to a luncheon there tomorrow, and I'd love to bring along somethin'."

This concocted story was aimed to discourage Melinda from accompanying her within, and it turned the trick like a charm. "Oh?" her companion said doubtfully. "Perhaps I will go rest, and have a cup of tea at the café, instead."

"I shouldn't be long," Doyle assured her. "History's not my strong suit."

"No—I'm not sure what is," Melinda observed absently.

CHAPTER 18

*O*nce within the library, Doyle paused in the foyer to get her bearings and then followed the signs up the stairs and toward the historic-archives section. It was a beautiful building, with its high, ornate ceilings and shelves upon shelves of silent books that hadn't been moved in many years, and could look forward to more of the same.

Which is an excellent example of why there's little point to preserving it all, thought Doyle, as she mounted the stairs. Someone's gone to a lot of work to put all these books together and arrange them just so, but no one's interested—it's a bit foolish, to try to focus on the past when the present is all around you, and sweeping you along at a breakneck pace. There's little enough time to focus on the present, let alone dwell on the past.

And—as was the case in any ancient building—there were ghosts in the rafters who watched her progress with keen interest, murmuring amongst themselves and jockeying for position so as to get a better look. She ignored them, and instead brought to mind what she needed to find out—she may not have a lot of time to get her goals accomplished, in that Acton and Reynolds could very well abandon ship in short order; only well-meaning men would think that a cathedral service was a good destination for a toddler intent on playing pat-a-cake.

Once she came to the appropriate landing, Doyle headed over to the reference desk, breathing in the distinct scent that always seemed to mark any library, grand or small. She wasn't one for libraries, but the scent was unmistakable—it rather reminded her of the London bookstore, that time when Savoie was giving her a warning, and Acton was smoking up a storm over that nasty reporter, may she rest in peace.

Her scalp prickled, and Doyle suddenly stilled. Oh-oh, she thought, thoroughly alarmed; I'm missing something—something important. I've truly got to find out what scheme that man is weaving—it's that "deja-view" thing, all over again.

Therefore, with renewed determination she approached the librarian who was manning the reference desk. "Hallo," she ventured.

The young man had been entering information into an outdated computer, but upon sighting her, he immediately straightened up and regarded her with a surprised eye. "Why, hallo," he replied.

He was a thin, earnest young man who wore round, rimless glasses and a skinny tie. In forty years, Doyle thought, he'll not have changed much. "I was wonderin' if you could steer me in the right direction."

"Of course," the young man replied. He seemed to have recovered from his surprise, and smiled warmly. "Anything I can do to help."

Doyle hoped he wasn't flirting with her—especially in light of her wedding ring—and continued, "I'm wantin' to research the Vikings."

He raised his brows. "Oh? What about the Vikings?"

"What language they spoke, for starters."

"Old Norse," he said promptly. "Very similar to the modern Icelandic language."

"Ah," she said. "Well, I'm lookin' to translate a couple of words in particular."

He bent to pull-up a program on his computer. "Of course— which ones?"

"*Dóttir*," she ventured.

He glanced up at her without making an entry. "Daughter? The word for daughter is *dóttir*, which is where the English word derived."

There was a small pause, whilst Doyle stared at him. "Fancy that," she said slowly. "How about *gersemí*? That's another one."

He typed, and then explained, "*Gersemí* is the daughter of Freyja, the goddess of fertility."

But Doyle frowned, and then slowly shook her head. "I don't think that's right—I don't think it's anyone's name."

"I see. Do you have any context, perhaps?"

"No," she offered bluntly, "I wish I did." She considered this for a moment. "Unless they sacrificed some poor girl, too—and that was her name? I suppose that's a possibility, but it seems unlikely he'd want me to dig her up, if he's already unhappy about the first fellow's bein' dug up."

The young man seemed to take these musings in stride, and offered, "The Vikings often sacrificed female slaves, for a Viking funeral."

Doyle thought about this for a moment, but then shook her head. "This wasn't a Viking funeral, though—it was more like a—

more a victory celebration, I think." She knit her brow. *"The blood on the roots amplified their power, and the man who died, died well."*

The young man brightened. "You are familiar with the *Hávamál*? It was one of my disciplines, in ancient studies."

Doyle stared at him for a moment, and then decided she needed to button her lip, else this fellow might think she was barkin' mad—that, or he would start quizzing her, which would be miles worse. "Yes; well, I'm fairly certain the word was *gersemí*, but mayhap he was referrin' to the goddess—mayhap he believed she lived in the grove."

"The Vikings believed the sacred groves were imbued with mystical powers," her companion agreed, warming to his subject. *"I cut runes of help, I cut runes of protection, once against the elves, twice against the trolls, thrice against the giants."*

Now I've torn it, thought Doyle, and hastily moved on. "Yes; well, there's another word I'd like to translate—*hor-loff*, I think it was."

"Hoffva?" he offered as he typed. "Hafa?"

She made a mighty effort to dredge up the memory. "*Herloff*? she asked. "I'm fairly certain that was it."

He typed, then cocked his head. "*Herloff* means trophies of war —something valuable."

Doyle's brow cleared. "Aye—that makes sense; he thinks the trees are valuable, and he's that unhappy that we've dug them up. He keeps goin' on and on about Yggdrasil."

"A sacred tree, in Viking lore," the young man affirmed.

"They watered the roots with the blood of their enemies," Doyle advised. "Human sacrifices, and such."

"Yes, they were merciless in battle—*I give him no hope of mercy; gold is little comfort for a kinsman dead.* You might say the Vikings were Ireland's original terrorists, so to speak."

Doyle stared at him for a moment, because she'd not looked at it quite that way, but it did make sense. "Faith, I suppose they were. A lot of bloody back-and-forth, over the years—Ireland's had more than her share."

"Very true," the young man agreed.

Furrowing her brow, Doyle mused, "I suppose that's why our terrorism laws are a bit different from the UK's."

The librarian nodded. "With good reason, after The Troubles."

And here we are, harping on this subject again, thought Doyle. Which makes me wonder if I should pay a bit more attention than I have. "How—exactly—are the laws different, d'you know?"

The young man considered this. "I think our legal protocols are different from most other countries. It's easier to be charged with terrorism in Ireland, and easier to convict. And it's done rather secretly, so that no one in the system can be threatened."

Again, Doyle frowned, because—even though her instinct was telling her that this was important—try as she might, she couldn't see how it pertained to the events that were unfolding around her. Sir Stephen was not a terrorist—quite the opposite in fact, since he was a "covert" killer and therefore something of a coward. Faith, the wretched man couldn't hold a candle to the Viking-ghost, or the Trestles knight—or even Acton, although it pained her to admit it. They were all "overt" killers, and not afraid to get their hands bloody, if they thought it needful.

So; Sir Stephen could not be deemed a terrorist by any stretch, and—aside from that home truth—there was one, overriding thing that should put her suspicions to bed; Acton had said he was not going to collar Sir Stephen, and it had been true. He'd not dragged them all to Ireland so as to trump-up a terrorism charge against the man, and therefore it was unclear why her mind kept returning to this idea.

Suddenly calling to mind another piece of this puzzling puzzle, she asked, "What d'you know about 'international famous persons'?"

The librarian leaned forward a bit. "I beg your pardon?"

She frowned, trying to remember—faith, she should pay more attention when Acton was spouting-off about something. "It was somethin' about 'collegial governors' or somethin'."

The young man ventured, "Internationally Protected Persons?"

"Aye," she said, brightening. "Good one. Do the police have to do special favors, if you're one?"

But the young man demurred, "I'm afraid I don't know—my specialty is history. But I believe the IPP designation stems from the Hague Convention."

Doyle gazed at him for a moment, then shook her head. "Not a clue, what you just said."

He smiled. "I can steer you toward our 'Government' desk; they'd know more."

"I'll save it for another time," she decided, since she'd best keep to the task at hand, and anyways, she needed to maintain her cover-story. "I came up here because I'm lookin' to see if I can make a copy of any old photos you may have from St. Brigid's foundin'—the school, in particular. I'm goin' to a luncheon there, and I'd love to bring along somethin' historical."

"St. Brigid's School was founded before photography was invented," the young man explained kindly.

"Oh," she said. "Well, d'you have anything else that might be pertinent? Everyone there sets such store on historical things."

There was a small pause, whilst he regarded her thoughtfully. "Yes, we may have some materials in the stacks. Follow me, and I will show you."

She duly followed him, as he walked past stack after stack of organized shelves—silent and rather forlorn, since most people were out in the real-world, and doing real-world things. "Not a lot of visitors, back here," she offered.

He glanced over his shoulder at her. "It doesn't help matters that it's rumored to be haunted."

"I could see that," Doyle agreed, since it was true. Although the ghosts here weren't frightening in the least—instead they were rather quarrelsome; taking great pleasure in arguing with each other over the smallest academic points. Say what you will about the Trestles-knight, you had to give it to him for keeping the other ghosts in line by knocking a few heads together, whenever he felt it necessary.

They paused before a locked door—looked to be a storeroom, of some sort, tucked away under the gables—and the librarian unlocked it, and then led her within. This room seemed much less organized, with unlabeled shelves piled high with stacks of large cardboard envelopes. He chose one such envelope, and slid it out carefully, unwinding the string that held the fastener. "Here's a map of the St. Brigid's area—it's a bird's-eye view."

Doyle gazed upon the antique map of the older area of town—the perspective all skewed, since they hadn't figured-out how to do it properly, yet—and smiled happily. "Faith, it looks just like somethin' they'll appreciate. Can you make me a copy?"

The young man slid the map back into the envelope. "You may take this one; we'd love to support the school."

Doyle looked at him in surprise. "Let me pay for it, at least."

"No need; it's been here awhile, and I'm just happy it will finally see the light of day."

"Well, that's grand—thanks ever so much."

"My pleasure," the young man said with a smile.

As Doyle descended the stairway with the envelope tucked under her arm, the young librarian stood and watched her from over the balustrade on the landing. Beside him stood a ghost, dressed in academic robes from a bygone era.

"Fah—she's oblivious," the ghost said in derision, as he watched Doyle's departure. "Hasn't the sense of a gnat."

But the young man immediately leapt to Doyle's defense. "Hush, you. She's out there in the wild, and that takes plenty of courage—I don't think I could do it."

The ghost sighed. "You can't hide away forever, laddie; someone's got to right the wrongs. You can't stand by, and hope that someone else will put a stop to it."

The young librarian made no response, and the ghost sighed. "I suppose there's no need to tell you that the latest Middleton manuscript is a fake, too. And no one knows better than I, since I was there when he wrote it."

Soberly, the young man replied, "But I can't say anything—don't you see? They'd all wonder how I knew—why I was suspicious."

"Someone's got to right the wrongs," the ghost repeated.

But the young man made no reply, as he watched Doyle reach the ground floor, and then turn to disappear from sight.

CHAPTER 19

When Doyle returned to the hotel suite, it was to find that the boys had already been fed and put down to nap early, and that Reynolds was scrubbing some sticky substance off Tommy's shoes at the kitchen sink. She decided not to ask too many questions, and instead sat down to eat her lunch, with her husband immediately joining her so as to keep her company.

"How was your outing?" he asked, as he lifted a chip from her plate.

"It went well, husband—although I haven't much to show for my winklin'—tryin' to get a straight answer out of Melinda is like tryin' to nail-down jelly. She does appreciate your efforts to put her feet on a better path, though, with tellin' her it's a good time to sober up and fly right. Very kind of you to make the attempt, although I don't know how much of it is goin' to stick."

"I am hopeful," he said.

Thoughtfully, Doyle paused to rest her elbows on the table.

"She's that fashed about Callie, and I can't blame her—I'll be dreadin' the day that Edward wants to hold me at arm's length."

But Acton, as was to be expected, did not wish to discuss Callie. "You have purchased a print?"

She glanced over at where the cardboard envelope lay on the kitchen counter. "Aye—well, not purchased it as much as filched it, I suppose. The librarian up in the historical archives said I could take it—have a look."

Acton stood to slide the print out of the cardboard envelope, and made a sound of surprise upon viewing it. "A Rocque," he said, frowning. "Extraordinary."

Doyle watched him as she took another bite of her pasty—bless Reynolds, for remembering that she fancied them; some good had came from their trip to the cathedral, after all. "Is it valuable? It's looks a bit off-kilter, for a map."

He continued to scrutinize the piece, his brow furrowed. "What were you told?"

"I asked if I could have a photo of St. Brigid's foundin', and this nice young librarian told me it was before they'd invented photography, but he'd somethin' he thought would make a good gift, instead."

Acton glanced up at her, and then carried the print over toward the window, examining it closely. He then asked Reynolds if he could borrow his reading glasses, and—after laying the print on the table, bent to scrutinize it through the glasses.

Doyle—interpreting these proceedings aright—ventured, "Mother a' Mercy; never say it's a *fake*, Michael?"

"Indeed. Come see; there are pixels."

She duly rose to go over and peer through the eyeglasses. "And there shouldn't be?"

He straightened up, his manner abstracted. "Not in the eighteenth century."

"I suppose that makes me feel a bit less guilty about filchin' it, then. Lucky I didn't give it to the nuns, though—shame on him."

Acton met her gaze with his own. "Do you think the librarian knew it was a fake?"

She stared in surprise for a moment, and then answered slowly, "Yes—although I'm not sure why I think so. Faith, he seemed so sincere. Michael—I'd hate to get him in trouble."

But he only pointed out, "The fact that he let you walk out with an archive piece would be enough to get him in trouble."

"Oh—I suppose that's true. It did feel a bit strange—I offered to pay for it, but he said it wasn't necessary."

"Did he know you were police?"

Doyle frowned at him for a moment, and then slowly replied, "I never said who I was, but I did have the sense that he recognized me."

Acton crossed his arms, and gazed out the window for a moment. "Say nothing of this, please. I will look into it."

But Doyle was catching on like a house afire. "You think they might be runnin' a rig at the library, and this fellow is hopin' to expose it? Mayhap it's connected to the fake-artwork scheme we caught-out in London."

"Perhaps. I will look into it."

She shook her head in wonder, as she sank back into her chair. "We are *truly* havin' a busman's holiday, Michael. And here I was that proud of myself for comin' up with the idea of givin' the school somethin' all historical, and such."

He tilted his head. "Perhaps instead, we can commission Javid to paint the school as it first stood."

Doyle brightened. "That's a grand idea, Michael. And we'll

make sure she includes the full orchard of trees—the Viking's that upset about the trees." She paused to knit her brow. "Not exactly *upset*, truth to tell; instead he seems to think it all very frustratin'."

Her husband watched her for a moment, his expression unreadable. "What does he find frustrating?"

"I'm not sure—not a lot of shades of nuance, with him. And it turns out that he's one of my ancestors, Michael—fancy that."

He ducked his chin to consider this. "I suppose much of Ireland has Viking DNA, somewhere in their genetic code."

She quirked her mouth. "He thinks I'm a bit dim, though—just like the Trestles knight does. Which is a fine turn of events, come to think of it—who'd have thought that I'd have my own version of the Trestles knight, lurkin' about in the family tree? I wonder who'd prevail, if it came down to hand-to-hand?"

"I think I'd rather not find out."

He was uncomfortable—as he always was when she spoke of such things—but to his credit, he would insist that she speak of whatever she wished; Acton was not going to lock her away in the attic, come what may.

She brushed an apologetic hand along his arm. "Sorry that I'm gabblin' on about it, but I was wanderin' about in the library building, and an old place like that always gives me the willies."

"Does Melinda know about the print?"

"No, she was in the café at the time. Although I think I've stepped in it; we may have to invite her over for dinner."

"Very well."

Doyle blinked at this mild response. "Well, that was easy—considerin' we barely survived havin' Davies over."

"No—I think it is a good idea, to bring everyone together in a social setting. I was wondering if we should arrange for a dinner-party with both Sir Stephen and Melinda, in an attempt to sort-out the Lady Madeline situation. Somewhere neutral, to put everyone at ease."

She stared at him in abject dismay. "Holy Mother of God, Michael—talk about givin' me the willies."

He tilted his head in an apologetic manner. "It would be useful to discuss Melinda's potential testimony, and to decide how to resolve the dispute." He paused, and then added apologetically, "I am afraid your presence is necessary."

This only made sense—he'd want to know if either one of them was lying, and so she should quit being such a baby and gird her loins—his precious legacy was at stake, after all. "Right, then; do your worst. Although Melinda could easily tell us one thing—with all sincerity—and then completely change her mind the next minute. She's not exactly predictable."

He nodded in concession. "Nevertheless, I do think it would be helpful to meet face-to-face, in a neutral setting."

This was true, and rather an interesting phenomenon of the justice system. People tended to dig in, when they could shoot arrows from a tower, but such an attitude was harder to maintain when human beings came face-to-face in the same room.

In all wonder, Doyle shook her head. "Faith, you're a peacemaker, now. There's somethin' I didn't have on my bingo-card."

"We shall see," he replied in a mild tone, which only earned him a sharp look from his wedded wife.

CHAPTER 20

That night, Doyle faced the Viking ghost again, and noted that he didn't seem as interested in re-enacting the ritual murder. Faith, she thought; he's gone all complacent too, all of a sudden—although I'm not sure why. It doesn't seem to me that I'm any further along in figuring out what it is he wants me to do.

"I went over to the Old Library," she began, "but I don't feel as though I'm any closer to understandin' what it is that you're tryin' to tell me. Save that we're related, apparently—so there's that. Don't tell the nuns."

"*Dóttir,*" he said, and eyed her sidelong with much amusement.

"Yes. And the nice librarian agreed that you think the trees are to be treasured—he spoke about runes and elves and trolls—wasn't really followin', but he seemed very enthusiastic about it all."

"*Gersemí,*" he said.

She ventured, "Yes—is 'gersemí' a person? Is she buried in the orchard, too? Or are you referrin' to the fertility goddess' daughter? That part seems a bit unclear—although to be honest, *everythin'* you say seems a bit unclear."

In response, he leaned back, and seemed to contemplate the darkness above him. Then he lifted his fingers, spreading them out in the now-familiar gesture.

"*Yggsdrasil,*" she offered.

"*Yggdrasil,*" he confirmed. "*Blót herloff.*"

She winced, slightly, and said, "Well, I hate to be the one to have to tell you, but your treasure-trees are slated for more insult; there's little to be done to stop the Heritage Ireland bureaucrats— they're goin' to be clompin' about like a cow in a cornfield. Fingers crossed they won't find much else—won't find this gersemí-person, if she's there, too—and then we can get on with buildin' the science-lab."

Again, he seemed amused, and nowhere near as adamant as he'd been previously, with his spear-thrusting and barely- contained impatience. She frowned, watching him, and ventured, "What's changed, my friend? You've gone all complacent, and it makes me uneasy—the same as Acton, who's gone all complacent."

But her companion did not respond, and instead began idly tossing his spear from hand to hand.

With deep suspicion, she noted, "And he's goin' to hold a peace-dinner, which also makes me uneasy. Acton's not a peacemaker—not any more than you are—and yet he seems so— so *helpless* about it all. He's pretendin' that his hands are tied, and that he's got no choice but to tolerate this investigation, but that's not my husband's m.o.—not by a long shot."

Slowly, she shook her head. "For the life of me, I can't make heads-nor-tails of what he's up to. And I still have no idea why it was so important that we come to Dublin—none of this makes a thimbleful o' sense."

Fairly, she amended, "Save, of course, that Acton would like nothin' better than to pack-off Sir Stephen on a one-way trip to Maghaberry Prison—that's a given. But I just can't see it—can't see how that's even within the realm of possibility. Acton's hands are well-and-thoroughly tied."

The ghost chuckled, as he idly flipped his spear from hand to hand.

Watching him, she mused, "You know, I've that same feelin'— the same as I had last time we were in Dublin. I feel as though I'm Abigail, kneelin' in the road before King David and tryin' to put a stop to the scorched-earth campaign that's underway. But that doesn't make sense, because there's no campaign—or at least, not as far as I can see."

Thinking along these lines, she frowned. "So; what do we know? We know that Acton would be happy to vengeance-murder Sir Stephen, but he's been stymied on a number of fronts. First off, he's got an Abigail-wife who's hectorin' him to put a stop his vengeful ways, and second, if he went after Sir Stephen, the man wouldn't hesitate to take the Dowager down with him—he's as predictable as the mornin' dew."

She glanced up at the ghost. "Not that Acton cares two pins about his mother goin' to prison, you understand, but he definitely cares two pins about Trestles and his stupid legacy. Acton's the placeholder, and he's not about to let such a terrible scandal blacken the history books—not on his watch."

She paused. "And third, he doesn't want Melinda's role to come to light. Even though she didn't technically commit a crime, she didn't exactly cover herself in glory, either. When all's said and done, I think he feels a bit guilty about Melinda, because she suffered so, at his father's hands. That's why he tolerates her."

Drawing in a long breath, she concluded, "So, it makes no sense that I've that 'deja-view' feelin' again—back in Dublin with the boom about to be lowered, but havin' no idea what the man's got up his sleeve. I can't help but think that history's repeatin' itself in spades—right down to the fact that he's makin' a nuisance of himself, and ridin' the Superintendent like a tinker's donkey."

Her continued watching her with no little amusement.

Slowly, Doyle offered, "And—lest we forget—there was another ritual murder, last time around. Faith, it makes you think that little has changed in a thousand years, despite St. Patrick's best efforts. Father Brown took a knife through the eye, and your poor victim took a spear through the head—and then was hung, for good measure. It's all very Old Testament, which brings me back to Abigail, kneelin' in the road and tryin' to put a stop to it all.

Her companion stretched out his arms over his head, smiling as though he was entertaining a very enjoyable secret.

Eying him with suspicion, she added, "And as a topper, it looks as though we've stumbled on another round of fake art-work murky doings, which means my work's cut out for me, because money-launderin' schemes are like catnip to my wretched husband. Mother a' Mercy, but there's no rest for the weary."

She watched him watch her for a few moments, and then said in exasperation, "You're precious little help, I must say. Which begs the question—why, for the love o' Mike, did you turn up?

And why can't I understand whatever-it-is that you're tryin' to tell me? I can't make heads-nor-tails, and whoever's behind this is definitely over-estimatin' my brainpower."

"*Dóttir*," the Viking said in some amusement. "*Gersemí*."

"So, you keep sayin'," she retorted crossly.

CHAPTER 21

*T*he following day, Doyle was attending the luncheon at St. Brigid's School, which ostensibly had been thrown-together to finish-up the ceremony that had been interrupted by the grisly discovery, but which was now serving as an excuse to put their heads together so as to discuss what was to be done about the Heritage Ireland people, and the grim possibility that the science-lab might have to be put on hold for the foreseeable future.

"Do we have any recourse?" Sister Mary Theresa asked Acton, under the cover of having a cafeteria-meal in the main dining hall. "I'm not certain who makes the decisions."

He explained, "All decisions are made by Office of Public Works, and it would depend largely on what is found, along with any indication that there might be other materials at the site which would invoke their jurisdiction. We are fortunate that there were no indicators in the grave; if it seems that the corpse was merely a murder victim of no particular significance, certainly there should be no need for any further excavation."

Delicately, the Reverend Mother ventured, "Is there a possibility that the Superintendent may not contact Heritage Ireland at all?"

"Unlikely," Acton conceded. "Now that the Coroner has indicated the remains are of ancient origin, protocol would suggest that he notify an exploratory team, at a bare minimum."

"He's a stickler, that one," Doyle affirmed. "I'm afraid that there's little that could persuade him to look the other way."

"It's that frustratin'," Sister Cecilia chimed in from across the table. "It's not as though the murderer needs to be brought to justice, after a thousand years."

"Nine hundred thirty-one," Doyle corrected, as she reached for more fish-sticks; faith, she'd forgot how utterly delicious they were, and she should make a mental note to start serving them to the boys on a regular basis.

Smoothly, Acton continued, "Perhaps we should discuss how the school should proceed if the project is indeed put in abeyance. I can make inquiries into the adjoining properties, in the event an adjacent owner would not be averse to selling."

There was a small pause, and then Sister Mary Theresa said, "Let's wait and see. You've been so generous, Lord Acton, but we mustn't overextend ourselves. Our goal is to be self-sustaining, and the future may not produce so generous a benefactor."

"It has always been our pleasure to help the school," said Acton, with a slight emphasis on the possessive pronoun.

Mustn't forget the placeholder-wife, Doyle thought with some amusement, as she crunched on a fish-stick.

Retrenching quickly, the Mother Superior assured him, "We are eternally grateful to the both of you, of course." She then turned to Doyle. "Have you heard, Lady Acton? One of our girls has qualified for the Sister Luke scholarship at Trinity. She's taken the test, and will apply at end of term."

Doyle smiled with genuine delight. "Faith, that's grand, Reverend Mother. Sister Luke would be that pleased."

With an amused gleam, the nun replied, "I'm not so sure about that—she wasn't very easy to please. But it was kind of you to honor her in such a way, despite it."

Sister Cecilia added, "And two sisters from the Order will be goin' to join Sister Rosaline's mission in Africa."

The Mother Superior nodded. "Yes; we can hardly spare them, but there's work to be done. Thank you again for your support, Lord and Lady Acton."

Good one, thought Doyle, as she decided that a bit more butter would not be amiss. Not that it matters a whit to me, but Acton has to be mollified; the daft man insists that everyone respect his placeholder-wife, no matter how many times she was reprimanded for sneaking candy into chapel, back in the day.

Sister Cecilia asked Doyle, "D'you plan to stay much longer, Lady Acton?"

Faith, now everyone's going to "Lady Acton" me to a fare-thee-well, thought Doyle, before she replied in a polite tone, "We'll stay for another week."

The nun shook her head. "A shame, that your holiday has been spoiled by all this."

"It has been somethin' of a busman's holiday," Doyle joked; "What with a dead body, poppin' up."

"Oh—oh, yes," the woman replied a bit hastily, and then re-addressed her dessert.

Faith, I should mind my tongue, thought Doyle, and not for the first time. But the strange fact that this has turned into a working-holiday only serves to remind me that I need to follow-up on why we've come here, in the first place.

Since O'Shaughnessy was seated on her other side, she turned to him, and idly asked, "You did a stint in counter-terrorism, didn't you, Robbie? I was too green."

"I did a rotation," he agreed, scraping the last bit of pudding from his cup. "I rather enjoyed it—didn't have all the constraints we normally have to deal with."

Maintaining her show of idle curiosity, she asked, "Oh? How's it different?"

He paused to consider his reply. "It's all on the hush-hush, mainly. A Special Magistrate hears the case, and you can hold the suspect without cause for longer than the usual."

Doyle prompted, "I understand there's no jury."

"No—not for terrorism. No one wants the possibility that the jury will be threatened, and so it's all on the quiet, and cut-and-dried. It's one of the only times the perp can be sent-in for a whole-life sentence, with no chance of ever gettin' out."

Thoughtfully, Doyle nodded. "And the chargin' laws are looser, here in Ireland."

"Somewhat," he agreed. "Given our history. Are you going to finish that?"

"Help yourself, Robbie." In truth, she was loath to relinquish her pudding cup, and she couldn't help but notice that she was voraciously hungry—especially for greasy, fattening foods. It didn't seem a coincidence that there'd been mention made of a fertility goddess in recent conversations, and so—with an inward smile—Doyle pushed her pudding cup over and asked, "How loose are the laws, though? For example, could you charge someone for terrorism if, say, they're Protestant, and they've up and killed an RC priest?"

He chuckled as he tucked in to the extra helping of pudding. "No, missy—they're not *that* loose. And you'd have to kill more than one—need at least two murders, at a minimum; otherwise the prosecutors would try to bootstrap every murder into a terrorist act, since it's so much easier to prosecute."

"Ah," said Doyle, and reluctantly decided that this promising theory seemed a dead end. Sir Stephen hadn't killed anyone else —at least, as far as she knew. But it was unlikely that he would; as Acton had said, the man was a covert killer, and somewhat of a coward at that. Not to mention the other roadblock; Father Clarence had been murdered in the UK, and therefore it wouldn't even be on the Garda's radar. Strange, that she kept thinking the terrorism laws were why they'd been brought here—there seemed little support for this theory.

O'Shaughnessy continued, "It'll be a shame, if the school starts crawlin' with historical do-gooders. I wonder how much damage they'll do."

Doyle made a sympathetic face. "I imagine Acton will do his best to rein them in. It's a shame that the victim wasn't just an ordinary victim."

"Aye—he's been lyin' there a long time. And here you were, swearin' on all the saints that you'd seen the perp on the grounds."

"Foolish of me," she agreed with a smile. "Just goes to show— you can't judge a book by its cover."

"No blame to you—once a copper, always a copper. If I'd of seen him, I'd of probably felt the same as you; no harm done."

"At least I got to meet the sketch-artist, even though it may have been a sleeveless errand for her. She's sent along her artist's portfolio, and Acton thinks she's very talented."

Immediately, O'Shaughnessy looked a bit guilty. "Oh. As to that, I may have stepped in it."

Doyle stared in surprise. "Why? What's happened?"

With some reluctance, he confessed, "I mentioned to the Superintendent that she was anglin' for an endorsement."

"Oh, Robbie; I didn't mind—for *heaven's* sake."

Annoyed, the man groused, "I didn't realize that he'd strike her from the list, sure as a shot. Stupid Paki."

"You mustn't be so prejudiced, and you'd think you learned your lesson with Miss Cherry."

Her companion immediately brightened. "Miss Cherry's aces. We're gettin' on like a house afire, and I may have to go to Londontown for a little visit."

"Now, that's just *perfect*," said Doyle crossly.

CHAPTER 22

*L*ater that afternoon, Doyle found herself alone in the suite for a few blessed minutes, which gave her a chance to root around for something to eat and think over what she'd learned, thus far—precious little, it seemed. Acton had retreated to the spare room—ostensibly to look into the real estate holdings around the school, but Doyle had the certain feeling he was getting his ducks lined up for this evening's dinner. The man wasn't a peacemaker—no way, no how—and heaven only knew what he was planning; she wouldn't be a'tall surprised if he was going to strong-arm his cousin somehow—or mayhap even Melinda. It seemed clear that he'd tired of playing cat-and-mouse —or whatever he was about—and must have decided to knock a few heads together before the whole thing spun out of control. It was actually a huge relief, in a way; she didn't like complacent-Acton much—she understood that fellow about as well as she understood the Viking-ghost.

The boys had been put down for nap, and Reynolds had

promptly brought over a steaming cup of coffee—the man was an expert at assessing her mood, bless him—and so she alternated sipping from her cup and munching on a bag of crisps as she lounged on the sofa.

Glancing at the servant, she informed him, "We're goin' out to dinner, tonight, and since Miss Cherry will have the boys, you're off the hook. Has Acton mentioned?"

"He has, madam. I believe I will take the opportunity to visit the Dublinia Museum; your mention of the Vikings has greatly intrigued me."

With a smile, she licked her fingers. "Happy to be of service, my friend—although from what I remember they weren't necessarily as intriguin' as they were ruthless. They were the original terrorists, in a manner of speakin'."

But Reynolds reflected, "I imagine, madam, that there have been terrorists since the beginning of time. But I believe what differentiates the Nordics was their philosophy; war as a pursuit of a man's legacy, with an emphasis on battle-tales."

"Aye," she agreed. "It was more important than anythin' to die well, and be remembered by the storytellers. Words were considered mystical, and so you tried to get yourself inserted into the sagas. *Cattle die, kinsmen die, all men are mortal. Words of praise will never perish, nor a noble name.*"

Impressed, the butler ventured, "I suppose it was a sure route to immortality, madam."

But Doyle made a face. "It was all a pack o' nonsense, my friend. A legacy of bloody deeds is nothin' to be proud of—the person on the receivin' end wasn't so very impressed, I promise you."

Philosophically, Reynolds offered, "Theirs was a warrior

culture, madam. It is a good thing, perhaps, that the world has evolved from such brutality."

"You should spend a rotation in homicide; you might take a different view."

"Ah." The servant bowed his head in acknowledgement. "You make a good point, madam."

Doyle nodded, and sipped her coffee. "Aye; it's a thousand years later, and there's still warrin' tribes who won't turn the other cheek for love or money—although usually it's because of money. There's too much profit, in musclin' people around."

Reynolds quoted, "*For what shall it profit a man, if he shall gain the whole world and lose his own soul?*"

Doyle smiled. "Good one, Reynolds. And speakin' of losin' your soul, Sir Stephen's comin' to the dinner tonight, which should make it a rare crack."

Reynolds paused in alarm. "Oh? I hadn't heard."

Doyle nodded. "Aye, he's comin', and so's Melinda. I think Acton's trying to get everyone together to discuss the criminal case—make sure everyone's on the same page, so that the Acton name doesn't wind-up bein' sullied in the sagas."

But Reynolds frowned. "My understanding is there wasn't enough evidence to bring a criminal case, madam."

"Not a case near Trestles, but instead Lady Madeline's lookin' to bring a case in Yorkshire, her home turf. You can prosecute a homicide anywhere in England, you know." This, said with the air of someone who hadn't learned this just recently.

Reynolds made a sound of disapproval as he returned to his tidying-up. "How distressing, madam; is there any possibility—" here he paused, delicately, "—any possibility that she would be able prove such a case?"

Reminded that Reynolds wasn't privy to the particulars,

Doyle only replied vaguely, "You never know, with a jury—they're both a blessin' and a curse. But it would be a nine-days' wonder, in any event, and so I think Acton's hopin' to keep a tight rein on it."

"A fond hope, considering who is involved," the butler observed, which was the closest he ever came to criticizing his betters.

"Aye, that," she agreed. "I'm not lookin' forward to this stupid dinner tonight, that's for certain."

"Perhaps Lord Acton could handle the matter without you, madam."

Again, Doyle was forced to give a vague answer. "No—I should go; it will set a different tone, if I'm there—they'll have to be civilized, instead of hurl insults." To expand on this, she explained, "When people are at war with one another, they tend to de-escalate when you bring them together, face-to-face. You see it all the time in the courts—they set-up mediation days to force the parties to sit at a table and try to hash things out." She paused. "And it works, a lot of the time. So; I suppose there's proof that we *have* evolved, since the Vikings."

"Certainly, madam—although I imagine the Vikings would be reluctant to parley in the first place."

"Now, there's a good point. Mayhap it hasn't changed as much as one would hope; there are a lot of people out there who'd rather double-down on violence when they're given any sort of push-back. And I suppose it doesn't help matters if your main concern is your warrior-legacy—faith, it's the opposite of Christianity, when you think about it. You'll get in trouble if you're not a scorched-earth warrior, whilst Christians get in trouble if they're not peacemakers."

"A very interesting insight, madam."

Doyle teased, "Once in a while, Reynolds; and rare as hens' teeth."

But the butler replied, very much upon his dignity, "I will disagree; you have your own brand of wisdom, madam, and certainly Lord Acton appreciates it."

With a gleam, she replied, "Mainly because he knows I'm an archwife of the first order, and he'd best walk the line or I'll give him what-for."

Reynolds did not deign to respond—mainly because no word of criticism would ever pass his lips when it came to the aforesaid Lord Acton. In any event, at this juncture Acton himself emerged from the spare room which immediately put paid to any further discussion; Acton didn't think it appropriate to include Reynolds in their conversations, and so she always had to switch hats, so to speak, whenever her husband was in the room. To be fair, Reynolds didn't think it was appropriate, either, and Doyle considered it a very high compliment that the servant relaxed, somewhat, when it was just the two of them.

Acton joined her on the sofa and accepted a cup of tea from Reynolds as Doyle asked, "How goes the property-hunt?"

"One parcel seems promising. I will make an inquiry."

Reminded, Doyle said, "D'you think you could make an inquiry for our sketch- artist? O'Shaughnessy's pulled a blonker, and mentioned to the Superintendent that she was anglin' for an endorsement. So now the poor thing's been struck, and I feel terrible."

But Acton only replied, "I doubt there is any redress to be had. She should not have made the inquiry during official business."

"Faith, you're just another soulless bureaucrat," she said crossly.

But he pointed out in a practical manner, "I've no jurisdiction, and I can't imagine the Superintendent would be interested in doing me any favors. If you'd like, I could arrange to have her added to the list at the Met."

Doyle immediately brightened. "There's an idea—if she's hopin' to be a real artist, she may want to go hang about London for a bit, anyways. We should keep her away from Adrian, though; I'm already terrified that we'll lose Miss Cherry to O'Shaughnessy."

He tucked her beneath his arm, as he settled back into the sofa. "I thought you were always telling me there is no point in attempting to control love."

"That was before love kept poachin' our staff," she explained, and then held the bag of crisps up to her mouth so as to shake out the last few crumbs.

"You've been quite hungry," he observed in a neutral tone.

Trust Acton, to have noticed before she did. Smiling, she advised, "I think it's a girl, this time around."

Chuckling, he folded her in his arms, very content. "Excellent."

She smiled, and ran a fond hand along his arm. "Speakin' of uncontrollable love."

CHAPTER 23

hey'd arrived at Fiddler's Green, an elegant restaurant that was situated in the second story of the Bettencourt Hotel, overlooking St. Stephen's Green. Acton had secured a private room, complete with its own bow window and a crackling fireplace in the best fancy-restaurant tradition.

However, despite the flowers and crystal stemware, the overall atmosphere was rather strained, as they greeted Melinda. None of them wanted to be there, least of all Doyle, who was never comfortable when there were strong cross-currents of emotion battering her from all sides. Faith, it almost made you appreciate the Vikings' way of going about things, which was to slay anyone who'd insulted them on the spot, and thus put paid to any festering resentments. Not that Acton had been insulted, exactly— more like Sir Stephen and his mother were reaping a whirlwind of their own making. It was quite the irony that—of all the awful things Trestles had borne witness to—it was these two nodcocks and their stupid, greedy plot that had wound-up giving him fits.

Well, not exactly fits, of course. Acton may not be an out-and-out Viking, but on the other hand, he seemed altogether more complacent than he should be, given the situation. Stay sharp, Doyle warned herself; the man's up to something and the Viking ghost seems very amused by it all, which is not exactly a good sign.

And to put an extra dash of icing on this cake of misery, Acton had disclosed in the car that he'd invited Lisa Davies to attend this get-together. When Doyle had expressed her surprise and dismay, he'd explained that he thought it might be useful to have the criminal lawyer present, to help strategize.

Doyle had met this disclosure with a mighty dose of skepticism, being as it seemed unlikely that anyone could hold a candle to Acton in the strategizing department. "But how can she participate, if she's just dumped Melinda as a client?"

"It is one of the reasons I've decided to make this a social occasion. She can socialize with Melinda, she is only prohibited from using any information she might obtain in a subsequent legal proceeding."

Annoyed, Doyle observed, "As though Davies would give two pins about the protocols, Michael—I don't know why you'd trust her to follow the rules. She's cut from the same cloth as Sir Vikili; even if her client outright confessed to murder, she'd somehow hand-wave it away with legal mumbo-jumbo."

"Perhaps," he agreed, and seemed amused.

Hotly, Doyle retorted, "It's not *funny*, Michael; the rules are there for a reason, and it's not right that the good guys are mindin' them carefully whilst the bad guys are takin' advantage of that very thing." She'd then pressed her lips together and decided to say no more, being as her wedded husband was much of the same mind as the bad guys.

When Sir Stephen was ushered into the private dining room, Doyle hid her surprise; she hadn't seen him in a donkey's age, and the passage of time had not been kind to him; his hair had gone almost completely grey, and he'd huge bags under his eyes—looked a bit bloated, he did. He also seemed a bit disengaged, and —taking a copper's assessment—she decided he might be on something; an SSRI, mayhap, or something similar. Not a surprise, certainly; he wasn't the stalwart type to begin with, and with Lady Madeline breathing down his neck it only made sense that he'd go the pharmaceutical route to soothe his frayed nerves.

Indeed, the pharmaceuticals seemed to be doing such a masterful job, since Sir Stephen went so far as to make a joking reference when Lisa Davies entered the room, and he rose to greet her. "Lisa. Come sit here; I can't imagine you'd like to sit with Melinda."

"*Dreadful* woman," Melinda observed, with a small shudder of distaste.

"I'm standing right here," Davies said with a smile, and then offered her hand to each of them. "Good to see you again, Melinda. Michael has asked that I come along to lend my expertise."

Acton informed the others, "Unfortunately, Ms. Davies is of the opinion that a criminal case could be filed as early as next week."

"I've put some feelers out," the solicitor affirmed. "The word is, they're going forward with all speed."

"Well, it's all a pack of nonsense," Sir Stephen declared, as he saw held Davies' chair, and saw her seated. "They haven't a leg to stand on."

Well, that's of interest, thought Doyle. He's truly not very fashed about it—mayhap Davies has assured him that the prosecution will never be able to meet the burden of proof. Either that, or the drugs are making him calm as a nun's cat.

But in this, she spoke too soon. "How is your mother, Acton?" Sir Stephen asked, in his insinuating way. "I am surprised she is not here."

There was the smallest pause before Acton replied, "She is well, thank you for asking. I will pass along your good wishes."

With an ironic smile, his cousin replied, "Well, if the trial goes forward, I suppose I will see her soon enough."

Fah, thought Doyle, as she struggled to keep a neutral expression. Now, there's a shot across the bow; he's reminding Acton that he's got leverage over him, and to mind himself. I should text Reynolds to go fetch another bottle o' scotch.

"There is still a good chance the trial will never commence," Davies assured all of them. "I will bring a variety of pre-trial motions before the judge, and one of them will be to dismiss for lack of evidence."

"Can the judge do that, without a jury?" Doyle asked, a bit surprised. Her only participation in criminal cases was as a witness, and so she wasn't clear on the overall procedure.

"Yes—the judge can decide there is insufficient evidence to even bring the matter before a jury. If the evidence does not meet a certain threshold, the case will be dismissed. To this end, I will demand an offer of proof."

"*So* upsetting," Melinda complained with a sigh. So much *drama*."

Annoyed, Doyle reminded her, "Lady Madeline's lost her son, Melinda. I think she's entitled to a bit of drama."

"Of course," Melinda replied, and cast Doyle a glance of apology. "You are right as always, *dear* Kathleen."

"You'd be that unhappy, if such a thing happened to Callie."

"I would," the other woman admitted, as though much struck. "I wouldn't be able to bear it."

Davies interrupted this rather alarming attack of conscience by saying in a brusque tone, "Lady Madeline deserves all the sympathy in the world, certainly. But that doesn't mean that I will allow her people to ride roughshod over my client."

"Hear, hear," said Sir Stephen, who then smiled as though he'd said something very clever.

"Lady Madeline's not going to listen to reason," Melinda mused, apparently still turning over this new-found perspective in her mind. "I wouldn't."

"I have every confidence we will prevail," Davies pronounced, and offered Melinda a reassuring smile. "The presumption of innocence makes a steep hill to climb."

"Unless you're a terrorist," Doyle pointed out. "Then the presumption of innocence turns into a molehill."

Davies looked upon Doyle with surprised approval, as though she were a child who'd said something clever. "Exactly—there isn't a better example of why the laws should never be twisted, no matter the incentive."

At this point, the wine steward discreetly knocked and then entered, and as he presented the bottle to Acton, Doyle found that her husband made a point of meeting her eyes, a clear warning contained in his.

Right, she thought a bit crossly; I'm to keep my lip buttoned, and stop blatherin' on about justice for fear that Davies may be alerted to the fact that I know Sir Stephen truly did poison poor Father Clarence—although I'd be surprised if she doesn't know this already; surely she's taken her measure of the man. But so long as she has no direct knowledge, she can play the game, and pretend he's as innocent as a new-born kitten.

As the steward uncorked the wine and performed all the nonsensical-seeming rituals that went along with pouring it out—Acton asked Davies, "Did you have an opportunity to inquire about the Dumont matter, Ms. Davies?"

There was a small silence, and Doyle was surprised to feel a sudden flare of wariness, emanating from the woman. "It slipped my mind," Davies said, with a smile of apology.

Doyle duly brushed her hair from her forehead in a signal to her husband that the woman lied, and also duly noted that the solicitor was hiding her chagrin that the subject had arisen at all. Now, that's odd, she thought; Davies is walking on coals about this Dumont matter, but didn't my husband tell me there was no such thing? It doesn't make a thimbleful of sense.

"A fine White Zinfandel, from California," the steward offered Doyle.

"None for me, thanks," said Doyle, who didn't drink, but rather wished she did.

"Me, neither," Melinda sighed, placing a hand over her wineglass. "I'm on the wagon—although White Zin my *very* favorite, and it *hardly* seems fair."

"You're not drinking?" Sir Stephen asked with some incredulity. "Come now; in light of the occasion, we should at least share a small toast."

"What occasion are we toasting?" Melinda asked in all puzzlement.

"To better days," Davies interjected with a smile. "I'll have some—thank you."

The wine steward began to pour her a glass, and then Acton said, "I believe I will join in a toast."

Doyle blinked, because she felt she'd gone through the looking glass—what with Acton drinking white wine—but the evening was to take an even more bizarre turn, as Sir Stephen suddenly leapt to his feet to wrest the wine bottle from the steward's hand.

Holding the bottle against him, Sir Stephen backed away toward the fireplace, the sweat glistening on his brow. "I—I don't think we should drink this—it's—it's an inferior vintage."

"Are you all right, Stephen?" Davies asked, her tone rather sharp.

Holy Mother, thought Doyle, as she stared at the panicked man, clutching the wine bottle like a life preserver. Holy Mother—

"I'd no idea you knew your White Zinfandel vintages," Acton offered into the charged silence.

"Well, I do—and this one is swill," Sir Stephen declared, bringing himself under control. "Let me call for another bottle."

"Not *swill*," Melinda protested. "Although perhaps not to *everyone's* taste—"

"If you would give me the bottle," said Acton, rising as he held out his hand. "I will decide if it is potable."

"A good suggestion," Davies said half-jokingly, as she stood in an attempt to wrest the bottle from Sir Stephen. He was reluctant to let it go, however, and the tug-of-war resulted in the bottle slipping from his hands, and smashing onto the hearthstones.

There was a small moment of silence, as the aroma of white wine suddenly filled the room. "Oh bother," said Davies to the steward "My fault; we'll need to have this cleaned up, please."

"Hold," Acton countermanded, and stayed the man with a gesture. "Nothing is to be moved; I am calling the police."

CHAPTER 24

*D*idn't have this one on my bingo-card, either, Doyle thought, as she found herself listening to yet another annoyed polite-war between her husband and the Garda's Superintendent. The man had been summoned forthwith, with Acton directing Sir Stephen and his solicitor to wait in the lobby, which had prompted Davies to counter that he'd no authority, her client was clearly drunk, and she was taking him home.

Therefore, it was Melinda who was sent to the lobby with Trenton, whilst Doyle's unhappy husband tried to persuade the recalcitrant Superintendent that he should arrest Sir Stephen for attempted murder.

"It was a clear attempt to poison the chief witness in the coming criminal case," Acton insisted, at his most autocratic. "You can certainly put the suspect on a hold, pending further investigation."

"I have no reasonable cause, Chief Inspector," the other man replied with a fine show of patience.

"You will; I insist that the glass fragments be tested."

"But we have no chain of custody, even if what you suspect is true."

Acton countered, "It was Mrs. Clarence's favorite wine—and an unusual one—but she declined to partake. However, when I offered to participate in a toast Sir Stephen panicked, and destroyed the evidence."

This is all very interesting, thought Doyle, as she watched him argue with the other man. Especially since it is very unlikely that my sharp-eyed husband forgot that Davies' wine glass also contained a sampling of the aforesaid wine. This is all a holy-show, for some reason, and so I'd best keep my lip buttoned until I figure out exactly what my high-handed English aristocrat husband is up to.

Acton continued, "I imagine the wine contained eszopiclone, or some other narcotic agent. Mrs. Clarence is known to drink to excess, and she is also known to take sleeping pills. I believe the intention was to induce a fatal coma."

Now, there's a lot of speculation in that statement, Doyle reasoned fairly, as she duly noted the skepticism in the Superintendent's expression. I'm not doubting that Acton's theory is true, but it must truly sound a bit fantastic to anyone who isn't familiar with the players.

Her husband concluded, "At the very least, all the elements have been satisfied for a charge of terrorism against an Internationally Protected Person."

The Superintendent raised his brows. "How so, Chief Inspector? You say yourself that you did not drink the wine."

"An assault was aimed against a member of my family, Superintendent."

A bit bewildered, the other man frowned. "But you said that your wife did not partake of the wine, either."

With a show of impatience, Acton explained, "The attack was directed at Mrs. Clarence. Her daughter is my half-sister."

There was a small pause. "That is a very attenuated theory," the Superintendent observed.

"Yet the protocol clearly allows for it. I must insist that the matter be treated with the utmost priority."

It's a bit embarrassing, truly, thought Doyle; and I'm getting flashbacks, watching Acton acting all high-and-mighty with local law enforcement. There must be something in the water, here in Dublin.

"I will call-in a forensics team," the other man said with some finality. "More than that I cannot promise at the present time."

Since the other man's tone was implacable, an unhappy Acton escorted his wife out into the hallway, where several hotel employees were pretending to be busy so as to catch a glimpse of what was going forward. No perimeter had been established, and —as the Superintendent had pointed out—they'd no chain of custody with respect to the wine bottle. Therefore, even if the forensics team found traces of a narcotic in the wine, they'd be hard-pressed to come up with a case against Sir Stephen. And if the lowly likes of DS Doyle knew this, her husband the esteemed Chief Inspector knew it even better.

Once in the lobby, Acton conferred with Trenton privately for a moment, and then the other man escorted a silent Melinda from the premises.

She's a bit shook off her pins, thought Doyle, watching her depart. Despite all appearances, Melinda's no fool—she must know how close she came to a bad end, here.

"I will have the car brought 'round," Acton informed his wife, but Doyle only replied in a mild tone, "No, instead we're goin' for a walkabout, husband, because you're due for a brow-beatin'."

But he was unrepentant, as he met her gaze. "I cannot apologize, Kathleen. Surely you could see what was happening?"

"Let's go," she directed, and he'd no choice but to walk along beside her as she passed through the front doors, and out into the balmy night.

They'd walked only a few steps when her husband said, "Let's hear it."

Annoyed because she'd the sure suspicion that he wanted mainly to gauge how much she'd figured out, she accused, "You set-up this whole dinner-charade because you knew Sir Stephen would likely take his only chance to kill Melinda. Up to now, he was confident that you'd sweep it all under the rug, but the criminal trial is suddenly loomin', and he's startin' to panic. Melinda's the key to his fate, and there's no love lost between them, so he can't count on her not to grass him out at the trial. Therefore, his best way forward was to silence her."

He made no reply, and so she continued, "And—knowin' all this—you pinch-pointed him so that he'd no choice but to make the attempt at this dinner; it's his one-and-only chance, since Trenton's been assigned as her watch-dog. And you knew exactly the means he'd use—he'd want to feed her narcotics, so that it wouldn't be obvious. She drinks at night, and she takes sleepin' pills. So, there'd be insufficient evidence to swing a homicide charge based on the autopsy findings—which is very similar to what happened with Father Clarence. Faith, they might even assume she'd killed herself, since the murder trial is loomin'."

She paused to take an angry breath as they walked a few steps and she tried with little success to rein-in her temper. "And because you'd a very good guess as to how he'd try to go about it, you told her she'd best get sober for this trip—which left Sir Stephen with a bottle of poisoned wine that you were goin' to drink—even though you don't normally drink wine—and since you're not one who takes sleepin' pills, there would be a clear line of suspicion leading straight back to him."

He still made no comment in response, and she covered her eyes with her palms for a moment. "And you were known to be arguin' with him, to boot. Mother a' *Mercy*, Michael."

"I thought it best to make it clear that I was aware of his plan," he offered, in a semi-repentant tone.

"I don't think that's the only thing, my friend. Much more likely that you were hopin' he'd implicate himself in an attempted murder—especially since he stands in line for your title, and would likely be appointed whilst your sons are too young. That's why you went to all this roundaboutation—you were hopin' for a clear case of attempted murder—or assault, at the very least—so as to pack-off the wretched man to an Irish prison." She glared at him sidelong. "That's why we're in Dublin, and don't you *dare* deny it."

"There seems little point," he admitted.

She stopped walking for a moment—she needed to catch her breath, after her epic rant—and they stood together on the pavement for a moment, as the sounds from people entering and leaving the hotel could be heard in the near distance.

"Michael," she scolded in a more level tone; "this was no different than police entrapment, and no matter how much you think Sir Stephen should be gettin' his just desserts, it's *wrong*."

"If Sir Stephen wishes to murder Melinda, better that I try to manage the situation," her husband pointed out in a reasonable tone.

But Doyle wasn't having it, and retorted hotly, "I don't think you're tryin' to save Melinda as much as you're layin' a trap for your cousin, Michael—no matter how righteously you dress it up. That's why you brought Melinda to Dublin, too; you were settin'-up a trap so that you could invoke this *stupid* famous-persons law, and try to take advantage. It was wrong."

"My cousin murdered a priest, Kathleen. It is not as though he didn't deserve to be punished."

There was a small silence, whilst she struggled to dismount off her high horse. "Aye," she admitted in a quieter tone. "But I suppose I'm more fashed about your methods, Michael—we're wanderin' into vigilante territory, yet again. The laws aren't perfect, but they have to be respected instead of bent all out of recognition so as to serve your own ends. The Superintendent was that gobsmacked by your brass."

He glanced upward into the night sky, and conceded, "I will admit that I may have overreached. But then, you must admit that Sir Stephen's arrest would have resolved many pressing problems."

"Well, let this be a lesson, my friend. Shame on you, for practically forcin' the man to attempt a murder—although it's all kinds of ironic that you didn't take into account our Superintendent, here, who's a stickler for protocol and not inclined to overlook nigglin' little things like chain-of-custody."

He bent his head, silent, and—expanding on this subject—she added, "And it's all kinds of ironic that you needed to bait your trap here in Dublin, when—as it turns out—you'd probably have had much better luck in London, where everyone bows before you."

"Surely not everyone?" he teased, glancing up at her.

But she was in no mood. "Don't try to joke your way out of this, Michael; it's not funny."

In a more conciliatory tone, he offered, "I understand your concerns, Kathleen, and—even as I may not wholly agree—I am truly sorry."

Eying him, she made a sound of skepticism. "Mainly, you're sorry that I've caught you out."

Since he couldn't deny this outright, he equivocated, "Perhaps."

"Well, Davies must have caught wind of what was afoot, too, and my hat's off to her for protectin' her client from himself. It can't be a coincidence, that she managed to smash the bottle."

He nodded. "I would agree with that assessment."

She glanced up at him, sidelong. "Save for her wine glass."

"A very good point," he noted. "Although I believe she lifted it on her way out."

Doyle frowned, as they turned to begin walking back to the hotel. "Why didn't you stop her from takin' it?"

"On reflection, the Superintendent's point about chain-of-custody is a good one."

But her instinct was suddenly telling her to play close attention—very unlikely that Acton would not account for any and all loose ends; it flew in the face of everything she knew about the man. Narrowing her eyes suspiciously, she asked, "What are you about, husband? If I didn't know better, I'd say you were soundin' like a first-year detective who doesn't know up from down. Why would you embarrass yourself so, in front of the Superintendent?"

"It was embarrassing, indeed. Perhaps my thirst for justice has clouded my judgment."

"More like your thirst for vengeance," she countered.

"You must admit that Sir Stephen is due for a bit of both."

Into the silence, Doyle blew out a breath of frustration. "Well, the point is this, husband; you need to do whatever is needed to take the pressure off, and settle this mess with Lady Madeline. You like to think that everyone's predictable, but they're not, Michael—not by a long shot—and you can't be certain what everyone's reaction might be. Poor Melinda may indeed have been killed."

"A very good point."

"And for heaven's sake, let Sir Stephen know that you're going to get Lady Madeline to stand down—whatever it takes—so that he doesn't go off half-cocked and try to murder Melinda again."

"I will," he agreed.

She warned, "Make sure Trenton's on his toes."

"Yes. Melinda's been moved to a different hotel, as a precaution."

She retorted a bit grimly, "I'm ready to move you to a different hotel, husband."

He sighed, as he drew her under his arm. "Please don't; I think I've suffered enough."

CHAPTER 25

That night, the ghost showed up and once again, he seemed far less inclined to castigate her about whatever it was that he expected her to do, and seemed much more inclined to lend a sympathetic ear to her complaints.

And Doyle had complaints aplenty, as she began in frustration, "It wasn't true, when Acton said he'd suffered enough. It wasn't true; he hasn't suffered—not a'tall." She paused, stewing about this. "I know the man like the back o' my hand; he's not wound-up, the way he gets when things aren't goin' his way—believe me, I've seen it plenty, and he's mild as milk, compared to that."

She paused, and admitted, "I've still no idea what he's about— even though I've been on high-alert for days. But he's up to somethin', and you need look no further than how he's not a whit ashamed of himself, for how ridiculous he looked in front of the Superintendent."

Nodding, the ghost made his "spearing" gesture—although he

seemed to do it more as a matter of form, rather than with any real ferocity. "*Blót*," he said.

"Aye; he wants his kinsman dead—that's the bottom line," she agreed. "Little doubt of it—although he's been made to look a fool, because he's been so—so bent on it. Embarrassin', is what it is."

The ghost lifted his gaze to peer at her from under his brows for a moment, before lowering his gaze again.

But Doyle insisted, "It's true—it's like he's clutchin' at straws, what with the 'important persons' law, and thinkin' this Superintendent's not going to know his chain-of-custody evidence. But he doesn't care that he looks the fool—there's a method to all this, but I haven't a gaffer's guess as to what he's about."

Her companion remained silent, and she blew out a breath as she eyed him in an accusatory fashion. "And meanwhile, you've gone all complacent, and I've a naggin' suspicion that it's because you don't mind that the Heritage Ireland people are comin' around to muck-up the school's plans. Is that it?"

Again, the ghost lifted his gaze to regard her from under his brows for a moment, before lowering his gaze again.

"Well, shame on you; the school needs a science-lab—modern-day girls need to bone-up on science to help them get ahead. It's not how it was in your day, where a girl's best option was to latch-on to some powerful man, and hope that he's the one who prevails in battle. We're miles more civilized, now, and shame on you, for siding with the stupid historical-people, and tryin' to put a stop to modern progress."

Warming to this theme, she crossed her arms. "The school needs the science-lab, and everyone shouldn't be so afraid to tread on old Viking-bones that they lose sight of what's important. Fah

—everyone dwells on the past far too much, and it shouldn't get in the way of preparin' for the future. As a prime example, you need look no further than Acton, who's desperate to protect his stupid family name from a nasty scandal, even though his stupid ancestors had plenty of nasty scandals of their own—people haven't changed much, in a thousand years."

The ghost suddenly grinned, showing his pointed teeth, and then made the "bicep" gesture. "*Blót*," he repeated.

"Yes, well, he'd dearly love to kill Sir Stephen outright, save that he knows I'd be that unhappy with him if he did. And aside from how I'd feel, he doesn't want anyone lookin' too closely at Father Clarence's murder and puttin' two-and two together— which they would, if Sir Stephen suddenly died whilst this murder investigation is going forward. So—it certainly seems as though Acton's shot himself in the foot, because now there's no way Sir Stephen can just sink from sight without puttin' the cat amongst the pigeons. Someone who doesn't know Acton might think he's been 'host by his own placard', or whatever the sayin' is."

The Viking-ghost threw her an amused look, his eyes gleaming in the flickering light.

Doyle nodded. "But I know different, and so do you. Acton's never been short-sighted one blessed second his entire blessed life. Instead, he's playin' everyone like a fiddle—includin' me. What's he about?"

In response to her question, the Viking chuckled and pantomimed thrusting his spear.

"Aye—laugh it up, you; you wouldn't understand, because you're a forthright sort of killer. But my husband's sailed mighty close to the wind a few times, and it makes me worry, with the last time I caught him smokin' servin' as an excellent example. A reporter started puttin' two and two together, and things got a bit dicey there, for a while."

Frowning, she gazed into the distance. "He always manages to avoid havin' the pillars come crashin' down, but it worries me, and it's half the reason I keep singin' the same old song and tryin' to get him to mend his ways. He thinks he's bullet-proof, but it's like those Greek plays—I forget what the word is—where the hero's own pride brings about his comeuppance."

The ghost glanced at her, as he deftly tossed his spear from hand to hand.

She made a wry mouth. "No; I don't suppose you can understand that concept—not a'tall. It was just the opposite, for you and yours; if your pride brought about your doom, all the better. Not a lot of hand-wringin' about it, so long as you wound-up immortalized in the sagas. Well, we will have to agree to disagree; I don't want Acton windin' up in the sagas, thank you very much, I want him home with me and the children—I'd not make a good warrior-wife."

Much struck, she added, "Faith, I think I'm the opposite of a warrior-wife; I'm a beat-your-spears-into-ploughshares sort of wife. I only wish I didn't have the sense that Acton just thinks that makes things a bit more challenging, so that he pursues the same bloodthirsty ends, but by usin' the proper means. That would explain why he's tryin' to catch Sir Stephen usin' Irish law—he's tryin' to do a work-around his law-abidin' wife."

Again, the ghost idly pantomimed thrusting his spear into a hapless body on the ground.

Crossly, Doyle chided, "You're no help, whatsoever."

CHAPTER 26

It was early the following morning, and Doyle stood beside her husband on the river bank in the light summer rain. He'd taken a phone call before the dawn broke, and then he'd tried to get out of bed without waking her but she'd sensed that something cataclysmic was going forward, and so she'd come with him—wishing she'd had the chance to grab a coffee on the way, since she was having trouble finding two thoughts to rub together, at present.

They stood silently under Acton's umbrella, watching as the forensics team carefully pressed the dead woman's white fingers onto the fingerprint scan, even though it was hardly necessary; there was no mistaking her identity—she hadn't been in the river long enough.

"I'm that shocked," she said quietly to Acton, as they stood a small distance away from the canopy that the investigative team had set-up over the site.

"You shouldn't be," he replied soberly. "You're the one who

predicted Sir Stephen was desperate, and might go off half-cocked."

"I thought he'd kill Melinda, though, not Davies. He needs her."

But her husband shook his head, slightly. "I imagine Davies informed him immediately upon leaving the restaurant that she could no longer represent him."

Doyle glanced up at him in surprise. "Because she knew that he'd made an attempt to kill Melinda? Faith, Michael, she could just hand-wave that away with some legal mumbo-jumbo; you'd have a hard time convincin' me that any of these high-level criminal attorneys are honest about the protocols."

"No; in this instance, she'd little choice. She knew that I knew what had happened, even if there would be insufficient evidence to prove it. And she dared not take the chance that I would file an inquiry with the criminal court bar."

Slowly, Doyle returned her gaze to the familiar proceedings that were going forward on the river bank, even though they weren't the ones who'd be following the careful protocols this time around. "Oh. Because if you were the one who was squarin'-off against her, she wouldn't be able to hand-wave it away."

"No. And protecting Sir Stephen would not be worth the potential repercussions."

Doyle nodded. After all, Davies ran with Sir Vikili and Denisovich—not to mention the Savoie brothers—and she wouldn't want to hurt her ability to milk those criminal cash-cows by getting herself disbarred for the likes of Sir Stephen. Nor would her dodgy clients want to be anywhere near a solicitor who'd raised Acton's wrath—she'd lose her clientele in a heartbeat. "So; she said she was goin' to withdraw from representation, and he—in a panic, and knowing how it would look—coshed her and threw her in the river."

"So, it would seem," he agreed.

Doyle shut her eyes, briefly. "Holy *Mother*, Michael."

"Indeed."

And meanwhile, she thought, it's my husband, who's calm as a nun's cat. Because he knew just how these events would unfold. I was wrong, yet again, and I never seem to learn my lesson; Acton smoked his way into predicting exactly how everyone would behave, in this little morality-play.

A bit nettled by this realization, she chided, "I know you didn't like her, Michael, but yet again, you've stood aside when you'd the opportunity to save someone."

"Not legally; I have no such obligation."

"The Church says you do," she insisted stubbornly. "You're supposed to step-in and stop evil, if you've the chance."

"Much of my job is spent doing just that, Kathleen."

"But not for her," she pointed out in exasperation. "You're not supposed to pick and choose—faith, you're supposed to love your enemies, not annihilate 'em."

In response, he asked, "Did it ever occur to you that neither my mother nor Sir Stephen was clever enough to concoct the Father Clarence murder-plot?"

Doyle turned to stare at him in astonishment, unable to find her voice for a moment. "*Davies* planned it? Holy *Mother*, Michael; why d'you think this?"

"Sir Stephen had approached her to explore ways to siphon money from the Trestles estate. I imagine the idea to create a 'Trestles Foundation' came from her own experiences with money-laundering schemes."

"Aye," Doyle agreed slowly, as the penny dropped. "She'd

know about such things back-and-edge—she's represented Savoie and Denisovich, just to name a few."

He nodded. "Often a charitable foundation is only a facade."

Frowning, Doyle considered this. "I suppose that's not a surprise, truly; Sir Stephen had lost his chance for any stipend from you, and it's not like he'd want to take-up workin' for a livin'. But it seems such a hare-brained scheme; wouldn't they at least need your permission, to create a Trestles Foundation?"

"I imagine Davies believed she'd be able to apply sufficient pressure, and I imagine she was quite pleased about creating an opportunity to do so."

The words hung in the air, and Doyle stared at him in abject surprise, yet again. "Blackmail," she breathed. "She's been around the other blacklegs long enough to have heard rumors about your doings."

He made no response—naturally—and her gaze traveled slowly back to where the forensics team was finishing up their work, zipping the body bag over the still, pale form of the late Lisa Davies. "She should have checked-in with Sir Vikili about how things tend to go when someone tries to blackmail you, Michael."

"I imagine she did."

She blinked. "Oh. The Dumont matter."

"Yes. An old case, from when Sir Vikili was a younger man."

There was a pause, and then Doyle said with some resignation, "You aren't goin' to tell me the particulars."

"No," he agreed.

"Aye, then; keep your secrets. But at least you did give her fair warnin', then, which makes me feel a bit better. And it seems clear that whatever Sir Vikili told her only fueled her desire to put some distance between herself and Sir Stephen—she must have been that relieved, to have an excuse to withdraw postwith."

He tilted his head. "Posthaste," he corrected gently.

"Thank you—posthaste. But then her withdrawal—and the circumstances surroundin' it—only gave Sir Stephen that much more incentive to want to cosh her and dump her in the river."

"Yes," he agreed simply. "Predictably."

She blew out a breath. "You're *somethin'*, husband. What's goin' to happen, now?"

"That depends largely on the Superintendent," he replied.

Aye, Doyle thought with dawning realization; that "Important Persons" kerfuffle was just to prepare the ground, so to speak. Now Acton's got a second murder, and so long as there's two, he can invoke the ordinary terrorism laws here in Ireland—he's on solid ground, now. But it still seems a steep hill to climb; I can't see how these two murders relate in any way, shape, or form to terrorism. It's like O'Shaughnessy said—they can't let a prosecutor invoke those laws willy-nilly, since the cases tend to be done quick-as-a-wink, and in secrecy.

And so, it would seem that Acton had hit a spot of bad luck, in that the lynchpin for his vengeance-scheme was the straight-edged Superintendent; Acton's dream of packing-off Sir Stephen to Maghaberry Prison did not seem any more likely, no matter how much he smoked and schemed.

CHAPTER 27

*A*t this juncture, the Superintendent walked over to approach them, his extreme chagrin hidden very carefully behind an impassive expression. "Chief Inspector."

But Acton was not going to be fake-polite, this time around, and said rather abruptly, "Perhaps you should have taken my concerns more seriously, Superintendent. It may not be my jurisdiction, but I am well-acquainted with the suspect and I should have been granted some deference based upon that fact alone."

That's interesting, though Doyle; my husband's comin' in hot, so to speak, which is only going to ruffle-up our Superintendent-lynchpin, here, and put him atop a high horse. Seems a very unhelpful strategy, if he's trying to somehow bootstrap a terrorism charge out of all this.

Her prediction was immediately proved true, as the other man responded in a clipped tone, "We are not yet certain that your cousin was behind this murder, Chief Inspector."

Acton was seen to bite back a remark, and instead bowed his head. "Of course. When you have completed your preliminary report, please contact me; I will share any information I can discover in the meantime. Is cause-of-death evident? Ligature marks?"

Almost reluctantly, the other man replied, "The cause of death appears to be blunt force trauma to the back of the head."

This was in keeping with a panicked attack, and Acton cast him a significant glance. "I see. At the very least, you will pull-in Sir Stephen for questioning?"

The other nodded. "Of course. He is a suspect, certainly; the wine steward reports that there was a scuffle between the two, and a broken bottle."

"Yes. If you would keep me informed, please."

But the Pakistani man only replied in a firm tone, "I am afraid that would be against protocol, Chief Inspector; you are merely a witness, in this matter."

Acton looked upon him with incredulity. "My wife and I know nothing of this, sir."

"I must interview all persons who are potential witnesses, sir; after all, you and your wife were among the last to see the decedent alive."

His brows drawn together, Acton stared at the man. "I must sit for a formal interview? You are serious?"

"Along with the restaurant staff," the Superintendent doggedly affirmed. "I must be allowed to do my job, sir."

"Of course," Doyle interjected, trying to throw oil on these troubled waters—the last needful thing was to instigate fisticuffs, here at the crime scene. "Only let us know when we should come in to the station-house; we can be available at any time."

The other man nodded rather stiffly, and as he walked away

Doyle hooked her fingers in her husband's elbow. "Come along, husband; if I'm to be interviewed, I'd best find out what my lines are, and whether you want me to throw over the table whilst I'm at it."

With a small smile, he placed a reassuring hand over hers. "You will not be interviewed, Kathleen; please don't worry."

This was as true as true could be, and—completely perplexed—she glanced up at him. "I won't? Well—at the risk of bein' snapped at—I'll point out that you're not the one runnin' this investigation, as our Superintendent here keeps makin' clear."

"You won't be interviewed," he repeated. "Although I will."

As this seemed a bit ominous, Doyle warned with some alarm, "You can't lie under oath, Michael. There's a Commandment about it."

"I won't. Instead, I have information that will see Sir Stephen immediately arrested."

For the third time this fine morning, Doyle blinked in astonishment. "You *do*?"

His gaze rested on the tree branches overhead, as he said with all complacency, "I do."

In some bewilderment, she frowned at him. "But you're not goin' to tell the Superintendent about it, here and now?"

"No. I would like the Superintendent to interview Sir Stephen before I say anything, so that he may take his suspect's measure."

Eying him, Doyle ventured, "Not sure that's goin' to help matters much, Michael—Sir Stephen's one who'll climb a tree to tell a lie."

"Yes. He is not a good liar, though—as the Superintendent will see."

This, of course, was true; whilst Doyle had an advantage in these things, a seasoned detective would be very good at reading the "tells" that indicated a suspect was lying, and no doubt the Superintendent would take Sir Stephen's measure in very short order. But—nevertheless—a homicide case could only be filed based on reasonable cause; it was often a source of frustration for the coppers, who would have a sure sense as to who was the guilty party but couldn't find sufficient evidence to bring a case.

Bemused, she shook her head as they approached the car. "You're not makin' much sense, Michael. You want to prepare the ground for the Superintendent to believe the worst—but he's the type to need hard evidence, no matter how much prep-work you do. He's goin' to follow the law."

"All will be made clear," he assured her, as he opened her door. "My promise."

And with that cryptic remark she had to be content. As they drove back to the hotel, Acton lifted his mobile to check-in with Trenton—listening, more than speaking, and when he rang off, Doyle ventured, "Don't let Sir Stephen get within hailin' distance of Melinda; he's a cornered rat."

"Yes. Trenton reports that Melinda has not emerged from her hotel since last night."

"Good." Doyle then debated whether or not to take-up her thankless task as a scolding archwife, and decided she'd best get to it. "You seem cock a' hoop about all this, my friend. Try to contain yourself—a woman's been murdered, and that's not a cause for celebration, no matter how much you think she deserved it."

But he was unrepentant, and pointed out, "Lisa Davies was a murderer. As is Sir Stephen."

"Aye. But you've got to let the system do its work, husband; that's why there's protocols in the first place—so that everyone doesn't run amok, swingin' a club. Might shouldn't make right;

instead, the community gets to hammer-out the laws to decide who gets punished, and who doesn't."

"Very sound advice," he agreed.

She made a small sound of annoyance as she gazed out the window, just so he knew that she was wise to his weasel-words. I should have known, she thought; after all, I know the man as well as anyone can. I thought he was just trying to get a bit of his own back—by letting his vile cousin twist in the wind for a while—but that's not his style; Acton's not a cat, who'd bother to toy with a mouse. Instead he's a spider, quietly weaving an inescapable web. And—as they like to say—vengeance is a dish best served cold. He'd cooked-up a plan to come to Ireland and make use of its unique justice system—no one knows the protocols better than he does, after all—so as to serve-up a cold-dished vengeance on a hated enemy. It remained to be seen how Sir Stephen was going to wind-up in Maghaberry Prison—none of this seemed within a country mile of a terrorism charge, and she'd bet her teeth the Superintendent didn't think so, either—but nonetheless, she didn't have the smallest doubt that it would happen; Acton was Acton, and you underestimated him at your own peril.

Which was something Lisa Davies had learned too late—not that she could have escaped her fate, of course. She was slated to be the human sacrifice that would achieve his aim—the second murder, because she was a hated enemy, also. It was very Acton-like, to kill two birds with one stone; he'd brought them all to Dublin to set these events in motion—complacent and unruffled—and then had watched as everyone behaved exactly as he'd expected. Small wonder he'd been smoking—the plan was foolproof, save that the man had a hectoring wife who tended to throw a spanner in his wheel of many works.

Into the silence, she said quietly, "Pride's your stumblin' block, my friend—just like those Greek heroes from the stories. You're not one to suffer insults to your high-and-mighty heritage, but, in the end, it's just words—thrown into history, and then forgot about. The Vikings had it wrong, thinkin' the only thing that mattered was how much carnage they could inflict so that the storytellers would tell their tale. That's the wrong kind of immortality to aim for; instead, we're supposed to turn the other cheek, and live in humble anon—animit—"

"Anonymity," he filled in.

"Thank you—because that's the surest way to immortality; or at least, the only kind of immortality that matters, which is hope of heaven. The truly great are the ones who pay no mind to the naysayers, tryin' to bring them down to their own, nasty level. That's what Abigail told King David, when she knelt on the road and tried to appeal to his better angel. It's a bit like you and me, Michael."

But he pointed out, "Abigail's motives were not necessarily pure, since David had vowed to kill her entire family."

"Whist, she was protectin' her own whilst savin' him from himself—there's nothin' wrong with doin' both at once. And it worked a charm; he took her words to heart, and then became famous for his compassion and mercy. It's thousands of years later, and the storytellers are still singin' about him—the Vikings would be that jealous." She paused and then concluded, "It's miles easier just to clobber each other, but we're supposed to take the higher road, and show mercy."

He reached to clasp her hand. "I'd only ask that you consider what would have happened had I been merciful, in this instance."

She sighed. "Your awful cousin would go free, and he's a nasty murderer."

"And that murderer would forever have a means of leverage over me."

She closed her eyes briefly. "Aye—I keep forgettin'. He could grass-out your wretched mother—or at least, he could threaten to. And in doin' so, he could show that you covered-up a priest's murder. Mother a' Mercy, it hardly bears thinkin' about."

"And so, mercy was not an option this time," Acton concluded, calm as a nun's cat.

CHAPTER 28

They returned to the hotel suite, and Acton had promptly gone into his makeshift office, no doubt to spy on the Superintendent and monitor what was happening—it was almost amusing that he'd demanded to be kept informed; Acton very much kept himself informed, and didn't need any help from anyone.

Doyle watched him shut the door with some misgiving, but her thoughts were interrupted by Reynolds, who reported, "Miss Callie phoned to inquire after Mrs. Clarence, madam—she has been unable to raise her on her mobile."

With a pang of alarm, Doyle pulled her own mobile to ring-up Melinda, but was sent to voice-mail. "Ho, Melinda, I wanted to ask you somethin', so phone me back when you have the chance."

She then promptly called Trenton.

"Ma'am," he answered.

"Is Melinda all right? Have we heard? She's not answerin' her phone."

"She remains in her room, ma'am. She called for room service, and I saw her accept the tray myself."

"Oh—well then, that's a relief. Callie's tryin' to raise her, but mayhap Melinda's gone to ground, and is sick of the lot of us. I can hardly blame her, after our latest attempt at a dinner-party."

"Yes, ma'am. I will let you know if there are any developments."

"Thanks, Trenton—you're a trump."

She phoned Callie, and debated what to say—always a crackin' minefield, made doubly so this time around, being as Lisa Davies' cold corpse had just been fished-out of the river. "Melinda's all right," she reported. "Acton has Trenton posted for security, and he says she'd stayin' in her room, and having her meals sent-up."

There was a small silence. "Why has Acton posted security?"

Now, this is exactly why I should think things through before I unbutton my lip, thought Doyle. Hoping to avoid tales of murder and murder-attempts, she offered, "He's tryin' to work things out, with respect to the Lady Madeline matter, and so he's just bein' extra-precautious." She paused, wondering if that was a word, but then plunged on, "Just routine."

There was a small pause. "Do you think Melinda's upset?"

Well, that's interesting, thought Doyle; I think I'm hearing a flicker of concern, here. "I'm sure she's fine, Callie—you know Melinda; she's probably left her phone somewhere and hasn't even noticed."

"Is she still refusing an interview? Maybe that's why she's not answering her phone—she's afraid it's the investigators."

"I've no idea," Doyle said honestly, and was suddenly aware that this morning's murder may have knocked the Lady Madeline investigation to the back-burner for a while.

Presumably, however, Lisa Davies' death would have little effect on Lady Madeline's raging desire to go forward with a criminal case—might even spur her on, as a matter of fact. But if Acton managed to get Sir Stephen arrested for Davies' murder, would the man still have to appear and defend himself in the Father Clarence case? She wasn't sure how it all worked, if a defendant was whisked out-of-sight, and into the secretive terrorism protocol.

"Kathleen?"

Doyle decided there was no bunkin' it—any anyways, the girl was going to find out sooner or later. "There may be a bit of a delay in the proceedings, because Sir Stephen's solicitor was found dead this mornin.'"

There was a moment of shocked silence. "Ms. Davies? Oh, no—"

"I can't say much more, because it's a pendin' investigation." Good one, Doyle.

In a stricken tone, Callie ventured, "I overheard Sir Vikili say something to Viday about how she was playing with fire. They must have known something."

For about the millionth time, Doyle found herself carefully navigating an Acton-minefield about what should be left unsaid. "Yes—well you probably should keep your lip buttoned, lass, until we hear what the Coroner has to say. Try not to jump to any conclusions, and I'll let you know first thing when Melinda calls me back."

"All right, Kathleen."

Doyle blew out a breath as she rang off, but she hadn't counted on the fact that Reynolds had been shamelessly eavesdropping, and was thoroughly aghast. "Did you say that Ms. Davies is *dead*, madam?"

"Aye—although I'm sure it wasn't the eggplant, so you mustn't blame yourself."

But Reynolds wasn't in the mood for gallows humor. "Good *heavens*; what happened?"

"She was attacked on her way home last night, just after we'd all met for dinner. I'll know more tomorrow; we'll get a Coroner's report, and Acton and I will go into the station-house to be interviewed."

"Do they have any suspects?"

Carefully, Doyle navigated a potential minefield yet again, and wished she had the gift of flim-flam like her husband did. "I truly can't say, Reynolds. But I imagine she'd a quiverful of enemies—it goes with the territory, rather the same as Acton."

Save that Acton's a sword-swinger, she added silently, and the late Ms. Davies was more of a sneaksby who liked to cause trouble behind the scenes. Mayhap the Vikings had the right of it, after all —saves you a lot of trouble, if everyone's afraid to cross you.

Bemused, the butler shook his head. "A very shocking turn of events, madam."

"We're havin' a busman's holiday, in spades," she affirmed.

CHAPTER 29

*A*nd so, the following morning Doyle found herself back at her old Garda station, seated with Acton in the lobby and waiting to be interviewed by the Superintendent.

As she gazed around the once familiar walls, she felt a pang of nostalgia; the old Desk Sergeant had retired—as had O'Shaughnessy— and now strangers were bustling about, keeping a sharp eye on the local precinct with the air of people who enjoy their work and feel that they are doing something worthwhile. The shabby offices where Doyle had cut her police-teeth had been renovated, and everything seemed modern and strangely quiet.

It was a bit disheartening, to see how much things had changed in the time since she'd worked there—not so very long ago. Time moves on, she thought; and nothing ever stays the same, no matter how much we want it to, and no matter how fondly we look back on what used to be. Nothing is truly within our control, and so—to counter that feeling of helplessness—we long for things to be certain and predictable; there's a great deal of comfort, in the sameness of days. But there's little hope for it—instead, everything is moving forward at light-speed and in the end, we're not the ones who are in charge. In all things, give thanks.

"Chief Inspector, Officer Doyle." The Superintendent came out to greet them in a semi-friendly fashion, which seemed a good sign; the man must have reconsidered his bristly attitude, and was now doing his best to make a show of goodwill toward his British counterpart. "This will not take long, and I apologize for the inconvenience."

"Not at all," said Acton politely. "We were among the last to have seen the decedent alive, certainly. Would it be possible to have a joint interview, so as to save time?"

Not a chance, thought Doyle, surprised that he'd even asked; protocol required witnesses to be interviewed separately, so that if they were indeed in cahoots, they wouldn't be able to keep their stories straight. So; either Acton was needling the man yet again, or he wanted the fair Doyle to be present as a truth-detector, which seemed a bit strange—surely, he didn't think the Superintendent would lie to him? The man was the pattern-card for a straight-edged copper.

"I am afraid I cannot grant your request," the Superintendent replied, hiding his irritation. "I must follow the protocols—you understand."

"Of course—it was just a thought. And I suppose my wife will welcome the opportunity to visit with her old colleagues, here."

Worse and worse, thought Doyle with an inward grimace; it seemed as though Acton wanted to remind the man that she was one of their own, and thereby put a thumb on the scale. It was not the type of remark that would endear him to the Superintendent, here.

But her thoughts were interrupted when her husband turned to inquire of her, "Does Officer Anwan remain assigned to this precinct? Perhaps you could have a visit."

This seemed an odd little tangent, but mayhap Acton was referring to someone he'd met during their last, best-be-forgot visit to Dublin. Doyle shook her head. "I'm not familiar with the man, Michael."

The Superintendent offered, "Officer Anwan works at the Garda station in Finglas, sir."

Acton lifted his brows. "My mistake. At the risk of sounding insensitive, I may have confused Officer Anwan with Detective Sahni."

There was a slight pause, and Doyle was suddenly aware of a wave of acute alarm, emanating from the Pakistani man who was standing before them. Mother a' Mercy, she thought in surprise; Acton's thrown him off his pins, for some reason.

The silence lengthened, and Doyle had the impression that the other man was thinking furiously. Carefully, he replied, "I am afraid I am not familiar with anyone of that name."

Startled, Doyle lifted her hand to brush her hair from her forehead—apparently Acton did need a truth-detector, after all. But what was this about? Something had shifted in the atmosphere, and the Superintendent was suddenly wary—wary to the point of being frozen in place.

Acton rose to his feet, and casually bent to retrieve his valise. "I might disagree," he offered quietly. "Shall I name more names?"

The other man crossed his arms, and then dropped his gaze to consider the floor.

It's for the cameras, Doyle realized; neither one of them wants the lobby feed to pick up that something very significant is going forward.

Into the silence, Acton said quietly, "My cousin is a murderer. A double murderer." There was a pause. "As I've mentioned, his first victim was an RC priest."

"Yes," the other man said with a quick nod, as he continued to study the floor. "You did make mention."

Glancing about in a casual manner, Acton added, "There may be a religious aspect to Davies' murder, also—certainly, such a thing could be explored."

The other man made no reply, but made a polite gesture toward the hallway door. "If you will follow me, Chief Inspector, I will take your statement."

CHAPTER 30

*D*oyle waited on pins and needles for Acton to re-emerge into the lobby, and was rather grateful there was no one she knew to talk to. What was *that* all about? Obviously, there was something in the names he'd mentioned—if they were indeed policemen in the first place—but at least one was; it had been true when the Superintendent had said the Anwan fellow was stationed at a different precinct. So; her husband was applying pressure in some manner—small surprise, he was a wizard at coming up with leverage—and it did seem as though whatever pressure he'd applied had turned the trick.

This conclusion seemed justified when Acton emerged from his interview; both men appeared subdued as they shook hands, but Doyle knew that Acton was triumphant, whereas the Superintendent was somewhat shell-shocked. As her husband ushered her out the door, no one made any mention of Doyle's interview.

The moment they'd come down the stone steps, she ventured in a low tone, "May I speak?"

"Of course," he said, and pulled her close with a fond arm.

"Mother a' Mercy, Michael, what happened? Will Sir Stephen be arrested?"

"He was already in Detention on a hold, and now the prosecutors will file a case in the Special Criminal Court. He will be then be transferred to an undisclosed holding facility."

She stared at him for a moment, equal parts amazed that he'd managed it, and annoyed with herself for being amazed in the first place; she'd been married to the man long enough to no longer be surprised when he pulled a rabbit out of a hat.

"What were the names you threw at him—some sort of code? Faith, Michael—whatever it was, the Superintendent had a conversion akin to Paul's on the road to Damascus."

"The names I mentioned were indeed police officers." He paused. "They participated in Father Gregory Brown's murder."

She came to an abrupt halt and stared at him in abject astonishment. Her husband dutifully paused to face her, waiting for her to recover from her surprise.

Last time they'd been to Dublin, Father Brown had been assassinated according to the protocols of an ancient vengeance ritual. The perpetrators had never been brought to justice, and Acton hadn't delved too deep, because—along with its not being within his jurisdiction, to begin with—it had been far better to allow that particular sleeping dog to lie. The priest's murder had been a case of rough justice being served-out where the system had failed the victims, and it had hit rather close to home, for the House of Acton. Therefore, Father Brown's murder had never been resolved—even though it had been clear that the manner of the murder would have required more than a few co-conspirators, since no victim was going to stand still and take a knife through the eye.

"Holy *Mother*, Michael," she breathed; "the Superintendent was one of them. "They were all Pakistanis, bent on vengeance. *Holy* Mother of God."

Acton cautioned, "The Superintendent may not have participated in the act, itself, but he was definitely aware of it, and no doubt approved."

"I'm that gobsmacked, husband," she said in wonder, as he took her arm so that they would begin walking forward again. "He's the last one you'd expect to approve of such a thing."

"Father Gregory had committed unpardonable crimes, and he was no doubt inclined to commit more." He paused. "And the ritualistic nature of his death served as a warning to others, who were so inclined."

"He knew it was comin'," Doyle recalled with a grimace. "He was that terrified—so terrified that he came over here to search you out, hopin' you'd save him." She blew out a breath. "Little did he know you'd be more apt to take-up a knife, and join in."

Acton, of course, did not reply to this home-truth, and so they walked a few paces in silence whilst Doyle tried to come to grips with this latest turn of events. "The irony's thick on the ground, husband; you reminded the Superintendent that there are protocols but then there are *protocols*, and he should remember what's-what."

"Something along those lines," Acton agreed in a mild tone.

And there it was—there was the lynch-pin that held Acton's plan together, Doyle realized; foolish me, for thinking that Acton's careful vengeance-plot was being thwarted by this jobsworth of a Superintendent, when this jobsworth of a Superintendent had been carefully chosen to be the one who would persuade the prosecutors that they'd a terrorist on their hands. Because in his own way, the Superintendent was a terrorist, too—it was all very symmetrical, as Acton would say.

Although it was still hard to believe that it had been so easily accomplished, and so she glanced up at her husband with a knit brow. "I'm that baffled; it seems unlikely that he can swing a terrorism charge where there's no evidence, Michael."

But Doyle's husband only replied, "Certainly, he can. Ireland's terrorism laws are very flexible."

Frowning, she made a skeptical sound. "I don't think they're *that* flexible, Michael. It's goin' to be hard to argue that he'd killed his victims for religious reasons—that theory seems a bit thin."

"A conviction is certainly possible under the IPP laws, Kathleen. There's little question that he intended to murder one of my relatives, and that Davies was killed because she'd become aware of that fact."

"Oh, right; that theory's a bit less thin, I suppose."

"I have every confidence there will be a conviction," Acton replied, and it was true.

He's got something else nailed down, she realized; mayhap the Special Magistrate will be one of Father Brown's conspirators too —I wouldn't put it past my husband to tie-up every possible loose-end. And small wonder that he's been so complacent, his plan to send Sir Stephen to Maghaberry Prison had covered all possible contingencies; "redundancy," the CID brass would call it —it was protocol to have a back-up plan that could be put into place if an original plan failed, for any reason. And so, Acton had invented two different routes to a terrorism conviction, depending on how Sir Stephen reacted to events. After all, he couldn't be certain that the man would actually steel himself to murder Lisa Davies.

Suddenly uneasy, Doyle realized she was perhaps being a bit naïve again, all things considered. If Davies was the mastermind behind the Father Clarence murder, there was little doubt that she was slated to be Sir Stephen's second victim, whether the man actually killed her or not—Acton would have made certain that the woman got her due, one way or the other. After all, Davies was another one who could finger the Dowager as being involved in the murder-plot, and Acton was never going to allow anyone to have such spectacular leverage over him. Sir Vikili had the right of it; Davies had been playing with fire.

Aloud, Doyle ventured, "It's seems so cold-blooded, Michael— that you'd set a redundancy in place, and then squeezed our Superintendent so as to make it happen." Glancing up at him, she warned, "No more smokin'."

"I have quit," he assured her.

"I don't know as you'll ever quit, my friend," she replied in all honesty. "But I'll keep kneelin' in the road, and hopin' for the best."

He bent his head to hers, and drew her to him as they walked along. "Surely, you cannot find fault, in this instance?"

Making a face, she replied, "I don't know, Michael—it feels the same as a police-entrapment scheme; you set it all up—and set-up all the redundancies, too. He wouldn't have been arrested if you hadn't done so."

He seemed genuinely perplexed. "And you fault me for this?"

She was forced to admit, "I suppose I've a hard time findin' fault. You've managed to give Sir Stephen his just desserts, but at the same time you've kept your wretched mother—and Melinda —out of it." She paused to verify, "They *are* out of it, right?"

"Yes. The Irish courts are not going to allow Sir Stephen to stand trial in the UK on what is essentially a parallel charge. It is important that the charging allegations do not become public, so that the defendant does not become a *cause célèbre*."

Doyle wasn't certain what this meant, but she knew enough to cut to the nub. "So, it's unlikely your mother's goin' to wind-up in the dock anytime soon, no matter how much Lady Madeline wants it to happen."

"Very unlikely," he agreed.

"You've saved the wretched woman's bacon," Doyle observed. "There's a small blessin'—however undeserved. I know you wove a fine scheme, Michael, but I will say again that it all seems mighty cold-blooded."

Thoughtfully, he offered, "Justice is often cold-blooded."

She quirked her mouth. "You sound like the Viking—and even though I haven't the first clue what he's sayin', you can follow the gist."

"It sends an unmistakable message, certainly."

"Aye—if you came after the Vikings, you had to be prepared to pay the price." Slowly, she shook her head. "But you're never goin' to convince me that such a message helps to keep the peace, because that's not the right kind o' peace—where everyone's afraid to make a false move."

"Not everyone is as fair-minded as you are, Kathleen."

With a sigh, she admitted, "Aye—I'm soundin' a bit naïve for a copper, aren't I? Fear of having to pay a price is what keeps most of the villains in line."

"Fear of reprisal is an important deterrent," he agreed.

"Which brings me back to how unfair it is, when the blacklegs can use their ill-gotten gains to pay high-flyin' solicitors to get them off the hook, every time."

"It does skew the system, there is no question. But there is little to be done, to bring about a cure."

"It's not right," she insisted stubbornly. "People shouldn't have to cower in fear when they know that terrible wrongs are bein' got away with."

"I certainly didn't."

There was a small silence, whilst their footsteps echoed on the pavement. "Touché, husband. Faith, I've been hosted by my own placard."

He pulled her to him, fondly. "I wouldn't say that," he soothed.

"The point is this, Michael; thank God fastin' that cooler heads tend to prevail, else people like you, and the Viking, and the Trestles knight would be runnin' amok and doin' whatever you please."

"Yours being the cooler head," he said, and kissed it for emphasis.

"Aye—although I imagine there are times when you are truly tempted to lock me away in the attic."

"Only if I could lock myself away with you."

She smiled. "That's very sweet, Michael, but I will say it again —even though it feels as though I'm shoutin' into the wind—that the proper protocol is to allow the justice system take its course."

"Which I did," he pointed out reasonably. "Shall we take the boys over to the zoo, this afternoon?"

She allowed this change of subject, knowing that there was little point in treading this tinker's path with him—he was never going to agree. And in the end, it was hard to muster-up her usual arguments—which was why, no doubt, he'd set this all up exactly the way he had; he'd a wife to convince that he was trying to mend his ways, but at the same time he was going to have his vengeance, come what may.

And—on that same subject—it was why she'd been thrown off,

even though her initial instinct—that he was going after his cousin —had been correct. He'd told her that he hadn't come to Ireland to collar Sir Stephen, and it had been true. But it was true only because he was setting-up all the chess pieces so that the Superintendent did any and all collaring. Faith, she almost felt sorry for the poor man; Acton had pulled-up his net, smooth as silk, and the Superintendent hadn't known what hit him. And now, Sir Stephen would be packed-off for a whole-life sentence at Maghaberry without Acton's having to lift a finger.

It was indeed an entrapment scheme, only this time the shoe was on the other foot, and it was a police officer who'd been entrapped by his own protocol. And not a paltry, police-rules sort of protocol, but an ancient, rather ruthless protocol that Acton himself abided by: you protected your own, and by any means necessary.

CHAPTER 31

*D*oyle was explaining to Reynolds that Sir Stephen had been arrested for Davies' murder, and—as was her usual state of affairs—she was having a hard time figuring out exactly how much to say.

"It was *Sir Stephen* who killed Ms. Davies?" Reynolds exclaimed, as shocked as he ever allowed himself to be. "Great heavens, madam; I would never have imagined such a thing."

"Goes to show that you never know," she offered, which was as ironic as the day was long in that Reynolds, himself, was not above a spot of murder if the occasion warranted, and he was a less-likely suspect than even Sir Stephen.

But any and all irony was lost on the servant, who was frowning mightily as he tried to process this latest cataclysmic event in what seemed like an ongoing series of them. "A love gone wrong, perhaps?"

"No—he doesn't love anyone, save himself," Doyle replied.

"More like she discovered something awful, and he was afraid that she'd spill the beans."

This hewed close to the truth, and Doyle decided that she may as well seed the ground for the coming terrorism conviction—not that anyone would probably ever find out about it; Acton had made certain Sir Stephen would forever sink from sight, as sure as if he'd murdered the man himself. So; mayhap it was a small victory that he hadn't—chalk one up for the hectoring wife.

The conversation was interrupted when Doyle's mobile pinged, and she saw that it was Callie, which reminded her—rather guiltily—that she hadn't got back to the girl about Melinda. Of course, all danger had now passed, but it was beyond the fair Doyle's powers to explain why this was to Callie, and so she answered in a breezy tone, "Ho, Callie—we still haven't heard from Melinda, but you mustn't worry; I'd have heard from Trenton if there was anythin' troublin' to report."

But Callie's voice was a bit worried, as she replied, "Well, I didn't want to bother you, Kathleen, but I decided to make the trip over to Dublin and check-up on her. I'm at her hotel, but I don't see Trenton, and the desk clerk says she moved out two days ago. She still won't answer her phone."

"Oh—oh, she moved to a different hotel, Callie—I'm so sorry, I forgot to tell you. But shame on her for goin' doggo, and makin' you worry so." With a quick calculation, she added, "Acton's workin', so tell me where you are, and I'll come pick you up; we'll both go give her a scoldin'."

"Would you? Thanks—that would be great."

Since Reynolds had been shamelessly eavesdropping, Doyle instructed the servant to ring-up Adrian and bring the car around. "Callie's worried about Melinda—which is a hopeful sign, I must say—and so I'll go over to the new hotel with her, and we'll have a visit. It does seem a bit strange that we haven't heard a peep."

"Perhaps she is indisposed, madam," Reynolds suggested delicately, since he had about as much faith as Doyle did in Melinda's continuing sobriety—and indeed, it wouldn't be a surprise if the woman had gone on a bit of a bender, seeing as Sir Stephen had been vanquished with the equivalent of a spear through his head.

"Mayhap," Doyle agreed—once again deciding that she shouldn't delve into any particulars, which seemed her fallback position, post-marriage. "I feel badly, though—I should have checked-in on her."

But the servant pointed out in a practical tone, "Surely Trenton would have informed us if he had any concerns, madam."

"Aye—I think that's why I'm not over-worried. Good thought; let me raise him."

She rang-up the security-man to ask, "Ho, Trenton; what's the latest, over there?"

"Nothing new to report, ma'am."

Not a chit-chatter, was our Trenton. "Has Melinda emerged a'tall? She's still not answerin' her phone."

Trenton advised, "I was sent out just this morning to pick-up pastries, ma'am. And as Sir Stephen has been detained, I thought there was no harm in it."

Doyle's brow cleared. "Oh—well there's a good sign, and at least she's eatin'. Callie's come to town, and the two of us are comin' over for a visit—we'll be there soon."

"Very good, ma'am."

Doyle was gathering up her things when Tommy emerged from the bedroom. "Paddycake," he announced, blinking sleepily with his hands aloft.

"Hold that thought," she told her son. "Your mum's got to run an errand."

In the manner of someone trying to distract a young child, Reynolds said with a great deal of enthusiasm, "Come along, Master Tommy; we will prepare cinnamon toast."

But this proffered treat only resulted in a more insistent demand for the pat-a-cake game, and Doyle quickly made for the door. "It's OK to put cartoons on the telly," she advised. "At least until Edward is up—these times call for desperate measures."

"Very good, madam."

As Adrian ferried her over to fetch Callie, Doyle remembered to text Acton, "Callie in town we will visit M."

As expected, he responded with "Shall I come?" which was very sweet of him, especially considering that he was no doubt monitoring whatever was going forward with the Sir Stephen case, and the last possible thing he'd want to do would be to visit with Melinda and Callie.

Loves me, he does, she thought with a smile, and texted "No need."

Callie was waiting in front of the hotel with her overnight bag, and Doyle realized they'd probably have little choice but to put her up, since it was unlikely that the girl would want to stay with Melinda. Ah well, Acton would just have to deal, and at least there'd be another victim to play pat-a-cake—Callie may have been a bit uneven, lately, but she'd always been fond of the boyos.

After greeting Adrian, Callie slid into the car, and Doyle quickly related what Trenton had reported.

"Oh—well, that's a relief," the girl replied. "Especially after the news about Ms. Davies."

Now, here's another crackin' minefield, Doyle thought, as she weighed what to say. Do I tell her about what's happened with Sir

Stephen? I imagine Melinda doesn't know, as yet, and so I believe the best course of action is to leave any and all explanations to my husband—which is something he deserves, after all.

Mentally wincing at her own cowardice, Doyle offered in a bright tone, "Well, we know Melinda's hale and hearty, so there's nothin' to worry about. She's probably celebratin', and misplaced her phone."

"What is she celebrating?" Callie asked with a small frown.

Faith, someday I'm going to think before I speak, thought Doyle. "Oh—oh; I think Acton's got everyone to stand down, in the Father Clarence matter. He's a champ at knockin' heads together." Truer words, never spoken.

With much relief, Callie exclaimed, "That *is* good news; I think Melinda was worried about it—or at least, as worried as she gets. The investigators asked me a lot of questions about her—about why Melinda didn't want to cooperate."

She didn't cooperate because my wedded husband was busy smoking and scheming-up his scheme, thought Doyle, but aloud she said, "Melinda's one who does what she wants, lass."

The girl offered a small smile. "That's what I told them."

Lightly, Doyle offered, "It runs in the family, mayhap."

But this venture was shut down in no uncertain terms. "I already have a family, Kathleen."

Mother a' Mercy but she can put that steel into her voice, just like Acton, thought Doyle. "Sorry—a'course you do, and small blame to you for bein' a bit prickly when everyone keeps forgettin' that. I suppose I'm just speakin' as one who'd no family save my mum, and so I would have been happy for heaps upon heaps."

There was a small silence, and then Callie offered, "I'm sorry I snapped at you, Kathleen."

"Whist," Doyle replied easily, and then little more was said until they pulled up to Melinda's hotel.

"Should I come up?" asked Adrian a bit hopefully, as he opened the door for them. He was hoping for a bit of Callie-time, poor man.

"Best not, my friend," Doyle advised. "Heaven only knows what we'll find—we'll need to check-out the lay o' the land."

"I'll be here, text if I'm needed," he replied easily.

They met Trenton in the lobby, and then the three of them approached the desk, where the clerk who was manning it greeted them with a discreet smile. "Good afternoon. How may I help you?"

Doyle informed him, "We're here to visit Melinda Clarence, but we're not sure which room." She paused, and—realizing this sounded a bit sketchy—added, "It's somethin' of a surprise."

The response, however, was polite but firm. "I'm afraid I'm not at liberty to disclose information about our guests, ma'am."

At this juncture, Trenton assured the man, "It's all right—they're family."

Inwardly wincing at the reintroduction of this touchy subject, Doyle quickly offered, "We can't raise her, and so we think she's misplaced her phone."

But the desk clerk held firm. "I must decline, I'm afraid—and Mrs. Clarence did phone-in to give clearance for her earlier guest."

There was a small, surprised silence. "She's a guest?" Doyle asked in alarm, her heart sinking because she immediately assumed it was Sir Stephen. But that was nonsense, of course—the man was locked well-away. "A gentleman?" she asked tentatively, just to make certain.

Now more certain than ever that he shouldn't grant access, the clerk said with a touch of censure, "I am not at liberty to say, ma'am."

But Doyle had a bad feeling about this, and pulled out her warrant-card, holding it before his face and hoping he wouldn't notice it was for London's Met and not Dublin's Garda. In her best police-officer voice she announced, "This is police business. I need to do a welfare check, please."

In abject surprise, the clerk bent his head to fumble for a key card. "Certainly, ma'am."

"Tell me about this guest, if you would."

As the clerk hurriedly led them to the lift, he explained, "An elderly woman, who was expected. She did not give her name."

Oh-oh, thought Doyle in alarm; there are two elderly women, featured in this nasty little morality-play, and both of them are bad news. "Was she tall, with dark brows?"

"No madam. Rather short, and grey-haired."

Not the Dowager, then; it must be Lady Madeline—Mother a' Mercy, but this was the worst possible news. She turned to address Trenton with some incredulity, "You didn't know of this?"

But the security-man only shook his head. "She must have come in when I was asked to go fetch pastries."

"Yes, that was when the elderly lady arrived," the man agreed, as the lift doors opened. "I assumed you'd been sent-out to fetch breakfast for them."

Doyle was now thoroughly alarmed, because it seemed clear that Trenton had been deliberately drawn off, and as they emerged into the hallway, she quickly texted Acton, "M's hotel 43." The police code was a request for reinforcements, and almost immediately her phone pinged but she sheathed it—no time to waste, if Melinda was in danger.

They'd come to the suite, and she asked the clerk, "Open the door, please."

"Perhaps we should wait for Lord Acton," Trenton suggested, since his own phone had started pinging.

"Stand ready," she firmly directed him instead, and he immediately drew his gun and took-up position to the side of the door jamb.

Nervously, the desk clerk stepped forward to slip the key card into the slot. "Shall I announce you?"

"No," Doyle informed him grimly. "If we think there's a hostage, we go in quietly—it's protocol."

CHAPTER 32

The door opened, and Doyle cautiously slipped into the suite's foyer, abruptly pausing in surprise at the tableau that was laid out before her. It was a sumptuously-appointed room, and at its center there was a large, silk-upholstered burgundy settee. Lady Madeline—or at least, Doyle presumed it was Lady Madeline; she was a rather stout lady dressed in mourning clothes—lay reclining on one end, balancing a glass of wine on her rounded abdomen. At the opposite end of the settee, Melinda also reclined, her head on a tasseled pillow with her own glass resting upon the floor, held upright by a careless hand.

Melinda turned her head to review the visitors, and neither woman seemed inclined to move.

"Hallo," Doyle ventured. "We were just comin' by to check on you, Melinda."

"*So* sweet," Melinda replied, and lifted a languid hand in salute. "I do so *appreciate* it."

The elderly woman gazed over at them, squinting owlishly. "Who're they, Melly?"

"That's Kathleen," Melinda said, and then added in the manner of the soppy-drunk, "and there's my *beautiful, beautiful* Callie."

"Oh," the older woman said, lifting her brows with keen interest. "She *is* lovely. I must say, they are not at all what I expected."

"Me, neither," Melinda agreed.

Lady Madeline waved a plump hand in invitation. "Do come and join us; we will send the desk for more pastries."

"The pastries are *delicious*," Melinda enthused.

"I've never had better," her companion agreed.

"Like *heaven*."

"I've had far too many, that's for certain."

"We are celebrating," Melinda explained to the newcomers. "It is what the Irish do, when someone's died—one last celebration. Isn't that right, Kathleen?"

"Aye," Doyle ventured. "We'll have ourselves a wake."

With a brisk little nod, Lady Madeline offered, "An excellent tradition—and so very fitting. It was thoughtful of you, Melly, to beg me to come over. Such—such kindness, such consideration—" Overcome, the older woman was seen to press a handkerchief briefly to her lips.

"I positively *longed* to meet you," Melinda confessed, her voice thick with emotion. "And—like an *angel*—you came."

"It was the very least I could do, dearest Melly."

"Have you been here, this whole time?" Doyle scolded in disbelief. "We've been that worried, Melinda—you weren't answerin' your phone."

"*So* caring," Melinda pronounced to the room at large. "*So* thoughtful."

"You are fortunate in your friends, Melly," her companion pronounced. "Although she has quite the accent—rather reminds me of my gardener."

At this juncture, Acton stepped in the door behind them, and was brought up short as Doyle met his eyes in warning and held up a finger—code-one, not an urgent situation.

Lady Madeline regarded him in bleary-eyed astonishment. "Why; who's this?"

Melinda waved a hand. "Oh, that's Acton, Kathleen's husband."

The other woman blinked. "*That's* Acton? Good God, why didn't you marry *him*?"

"It's rather a long story," Melinda said vaguely.

"Because I married him, instead," Doyle replied a bit tartly. "And Melinda, here—lest we forget—married your son."

"God's ways are *undivinable*," Melinda observed, and took a sip of her wine.

"Amen," Lady Madeline agreed, as tears again filled her eyes. "And I know you made him so happy, Melly—so happy—" she paused, and then—her voice quavering a bit—she said to Acton, "Do you mind, sir, if I do not rise to greet you? We are not standing on ceremony, as you see."

"Not at all," Acton replied politely, and bowed his head. "A pleasure."

"Such charming manners," Lady Madeline sighed. "Such *presence*." As though reminded, she said to Melinda, "We must find you another husband, Melly. A kind, sensitive woman like you should not be alone."

"Not Acton," Doyle said firmly

"I will never marry again," Melinda proclaimed with quiet dignity. "No one could ever take Herbert's place."

"Egbert," Lady Madeline corrected gently.

"*Such* a wonderful man."

"A saint," Lady Madeline agreed sadly. "Few could see it."

"I could," Melinda assured her. "He was so *good.*"

"I can see why he loved you, Melly."

The two women lapsed into sentimental silence, and Doyle decided she may as well take advantage of the fact that Lady Madeline was drunk as a fiddler. "I'm that sorry your son's dead, Lady Madeline; he was indeed a good man. But you're drivin' everyone mad, and I can't think he'd like that as his legacy."

"Yes," Lady Madeline agreed tearfully. "Oh—you are so right, Kathleen. And dearest Melly has been suffering for it, poor thing."

"I have," Melinda offered sadly. "I miss him so."

"If only I'd come to meet you sooner," the older woman admitted with all remorse. "So many misunderstandings would have been avoided."

"And you would have met Callie, too," Melinda said, indicating the girl with a negligent hand. "After all, she's your granddaughter."

There was a small silence, and then—slowly—Lady Madeline propped herself up on her elbows, as she stared, bleary-eyed, at the younger girl. "Blessed St. Mary; so she is."

"I suppose that's true," Callie agreed in some bemusement. "Your step-grandaughter, in any event."

"A miracle," the older woman breathed, her face brightening. "In the teeth of despair; a miracle."

"We should bring her to Paris with us," Melinda suggested, as though the idea had just occurred to her.

But this plan was promptly scotched by the older woman. "Oh

—nonsense, Melly; let her be. A pretty young thing doesn't want to wash about with the likes of us."

Callie ventured, "I don't think I can go to Paris, just now. I'm going to start classes at university."

"And she has a new beau," Melinda disclosed in a stage whisper. "A very attractive fellow—*so* much better than the last one."

"I must meet him," Lady Madeline pronounced. "It is my duty to see dear Callie well-settled. Has she a decent dowry?"

"Are you two goin' to Paris?" Doyle interrupted, so that Callie wouldn't bristle at this high-handedness.

"Immediately," Melinda affirmed. "Lady M needs to travel, and take her mind off her grief."

"It's your grief, too, Melly—a shared grief, between us."

"We are going to be gay," Melinda instructed the older woman firmly. "We are going to drink champagne, and dance with handsome men—Egbert would have wanted us to."

"Oh—oh, then I shall need a new hat," Lady Madeline pronounced, much struck.

Melinda addressed Callie. "Could you spare us an hour's hat-shopping, *dearest, dearest* Callie?"

"Of course," said Callie, who was very quick on the uptake.

"You will need a new hat anyway, for university," Lady Madeline informed her, and then added archly, "And for your new beau."

Doyle braced for impact, but to her surprise, the girl only replied in a mild tone, "I suppose I do."

Since this seemed an opportune time to make an exit, Doyle declared in a hearty tone, "All's well that ends well, then. D'you mind if Acton and I leave the three of you?"

"Oh—not at all, Kathleen. So good to meet you; Melly has told me so much."

Melinda teased, "Don't give her any money, Lady M—Acton's got more than enough."

"We shall see," the older woman replied in an arch tone, and then held out a hand to address Callie. "Would you mind bringing over that box of chocolates on the table, dear?"

CHAPTER 33

*D*oyle could barely contain herself until they'd emerged from the hotel's front doors, and then she promptly started laughing. "Faith, Michael; I don't know whether I'm afoot or horseback. Leave it to Melinda, to pull the rug out—she saw where all this was headin', and decided to cut everyone off at the knees."

Her husband smiled, genuinely amused. "A very interesting turn of events."

"Faith, mayhap you should have married her, after all—she's miles more wily than the likes of me."

There was a small pause. "Perish the thought."

Oh, Doyle realized; I've truly got to think, before I say whatever crosses my mind; his wretched father made certain that those two would never have a future. Quickly, she added, "And Callie was willin' to play her part—good on her."

"Yes. It does seem as though she is making more of an effort, lately."

"Well, she came all the way over here to check on Melinda, which seems promisin'. We just needed a bit o' patience, Michael."

"You have been more patient than I, certainly."

Doyle made a wry mouth. "I'm just the Abigail, tryin' to save my people despite everyone's tendency to run amok. And when you think about it, Melinda's an Abigail, too—willin' to kneel in the road and appeal to Lady Madeline's better angel. Abigails are thick on the ground, in this sorry tale."

With a smile, he drew her to him, as they headed to his car. "An epic tale, replete with Vikings."

"Aye, their storytellers would love the repleteness of it," she agreed. "There's a family at war, and betrayals, and pride, and envy—and nearly every other deadly sin you can think of." She considered this for a moment. "Not lust, though—unless you count you and me."

"I might disagree," he said, as he opened the car door for her. "I believe Father Clarence represents lust."

As she slid in, she laughed. "Oh—that's right. Don't remind me; it gives me the willies, to think that a priest would succumb."

"Melinda can be very persuasive, certainly."

Doyle suddenly sobered, and stayed his hand before he closed the car door. "She's a bit wounded, Michael. Still."

"I know," he agreed quietly.

Gently, she ventured, "So are you."

She wasn't sure he'd answer, but he looked away for a moment, and then replied, "A thousand times better, since I met you."

With quiet sincerity, she said, "We can't let your father's legacy dictate our future, Michael—it's over and done with. I think that's half the reason you're so unhappy with Callie—she's a living reminder of the wretched man. But we're not supposed to visit the sins of the father upon the children; our legacy is our own to make, and no one starts out with a black mark. None of this is her fault, any more than it's yours."

He took a breath, and contemplated the horizon again. "It is not such a simple thing to forget, Kathleen."

"Aye—I don't know how I'd even try to go about it, were I in your shoes."

She decided to close the topic—she'd a fine-tuned radar, when it came to how much to press him—and so she released his hand and concluded, "I only hope this little episode will help Melinda and Callie come to better terms—it would go a long ways to close that chapter, I think."

"Yes. And all the more reason to be grateful that Sir Stephen will never be a defendant in a public case."

He closed the car door, and as he came around to the driver's side, Doyle sat in silent surprise, staring out the windscreen with unseeing eyes. *Of course*—Holy Mother, of course. She hadn't thought about that aspect of it, but *of course* Acton would be hell-bent on making certain that Sir Stephen never took the stand in a public trial; the man should never be given an opportunity to expose the whole tawdry tale about Acton's father. Because he would, of course; he'd have been a cornered rat, if he'd been named in a public murder trial, and he would have used whatever leverage he could.

So; not only did her husband pull-up his net on the Superintendent, he'd also pulled-up his net on Sir Stephen, who'd no doubt been counting on this particular ace-up-his-sleeve. He was going threaten to reveal all, and force Acton to make everyone stand down so as to protect the House of Acton's precious heritage—it would be another leaf of blackmail on her husband, only with *miles* more leverage than the paltry cover-up of a priest's murder. And Acton wouldn't have had much choice but to knuckle-under to his hated cousin—his legacy meant everything to him.

But now—now Sir Stephen would never even be given the chance to blackmail Acton into doing his bidding. Because—as Sir Vikili and Lisa Davies had also discovered—you didn't go at Acton, and not be made to pay a terrible price. A lesson Sir Stephen would have many bleak years to contemplate.

When her husband started-up the car, Doyle decided that she may as well ask, "If Melinda hadn't saved the day, what would you have done about Lady Madeline?" It went without saying that he'd a plan to scotch her plan—it would be child's play, compared to swinging a terrorism charge where there wasn't one.

His answer came readily. "I would have threatened a civil countersuit, alleging that Father Clarence perpetrated a fraud with the intent of siphoning money from my estate. I imagine the entire matter would have been promptly dropped."

"Yes," Doyle agreed thoughtfully. "Lady Madeline wouldn't have wanted her son's legacy desmirched."

"Indeed."

Having caught a quick flare of amusement, she accused, "You know, Michael, I am startin' to suspect that you've decided to stop correctin' me."

"I like the way you speak," he replied. "And everyone else may be damned."

"Fair enough," she agreed with a smile. "So now, what do we tell everyone about Sir Stephen?"

In an even tone, he replied, "I would prefer that we never discuss Sir Stephen again."

She nodded slightly, as she reviewed the passing scenery. "All right—he's been stricken from the saga. You know, that's exactly what Njáll Hámondarson did to Gunnar, when the foolish man came at his brother in battle."

There was a small pause. "I am afraid I am not familiar with him."

"You should be," she observed. "It's like the two of you are peas in a pod."

CHAPTER 34

oyle was standing with the Mother Superior and Sister Cecelia, as the three women rather glumly watched the two representatives from Heritage Ireland mark-off various portions of the former orchard. True to form, the Superintendent had felt compelled to report the corpse's age, and now the school's science-lab project had come to a crashing halt so that sample excavations could be done—the aim to determine whether the site was a potential candidate for protection under the Heritage Act.

Doyle was pleased to see that the librarian from Trinity College had been included as part of the initial assessment committee, and she greeted him warmly. She felt a kinship with the man, with his being so shy—rather like she was, way back when she'd gone to school here, and dreamed of greater things.

She was soon to realize that his presence wasn't happenstance, however, when her husband casually engaged the man in quiet conversation. So; she thought; Acton must have asked for him to be included, and is using this as an excuse to question the librarian about the fake map; leave it to my husband to put this stupid excavation project to good use.

Watching the two representatives as they conferred, Sister Maria Theresa sighed. "Such a shame. Not that their work isn't important, but ours is, too."

"Aye," Doyle agreed. "But these types never seem to think so; the past is miles more important to them than the future. They have it all backwards."

"They are tryin' to preserve Ireland's historical legacy," Sister Cecilia offered. "And I suppose 'tis important to understand what happened in history, so that we don't make the same mistakes."

"May as well bark at the moon, Sister," Doyle replied in a dry tone. "Human nature hasn't changed much in thousands of years, believe you me."

In response to this worldly bit of cynicism, Sister Mary Theresa quoted, *"So we will fix our eyes not on what is seen, but on what is unseen, since what is seen is temporary, but what is unseen is eternal."*

Sister Cecilia chuckled, and Doyle smiled. "Amen."

They continued to watch the proceedings, and Doyle was reminded that the Viking-ghost hadn't come around to see her these past two nights; it did seem as though his attitude had changed from the first time she'd met him, though, in that he'd seemed less bent on explaining to her whatever-it-was she was supposed to understand these past couple of visits, and had seemed miles more complacent. It almost seemed as though his attitude changed once the bureaucrats had decided to dig-up more of his precious trees—he'd washed his hands and given up, mayhap. It was just as well; having to handle one fearsome man was more than enough, thank you very much.

On the other hand, she'd obviously made some headway with her own fearsome-man-in-residence, and so mayhap she could take some comfort in that. The old Acton would have gone after Sir Stephen breathing fire, but the wife-pleasing Acton had gone about it properly and within the bounds of the law—even if it was all an elaborate entrapment scheme so as to stick the man in Maghaberry on a permanent visit. Ah well; best take whatever victories she may—at least he'd made a show of following the protocols, this time around.

And—think of the devil and up he pops—her fearsome husband now approached her, having accomplished whatever he'd wanted to accomplish with the librarian. He came to stand by her side as they watched the representatives discuss the task at hand with no urgency whatsoever, and Doyle was moved to say, "It's all very ironic, husband; you can swing a terrorism conviction on the flimsiest of grounds, but you're no match for the wretched bureaucrats, who would rather die a thousand deaths than leave well enough alone."

"Very disappointing," he agreed, as they watched the two men engage in an extended discussion about which measuring implement would be the best one to use. "Although we can hope their assessment will be a short one; there's been little to excite interest, so far."

But Doyle only made a face. "Perish the thought, husband; they're gettin' paid no matter how long it takes, and with no end in mind. It will take forever."

They observed the proceedings for a few more minutes, and then Doyle sighed. "This is too painful to watch, and we'd best get the boys out of their hair, I suppose. We can go over for another spell at the playground, if you're willin'."

Acton walked over to take their leave of the nuns whilst Doyle went to gather-up her sons—save that there was no need, because the two little boys were in the process of racing over to her.

"Mum," said Edward excitedly. "Tommy's found something."

Since the last thing Tommy found was a dead lizard, Doyle held her distance. "Show me what you've found, Tommy."

Proudly, the little boy opened his hand, to reveal a gold-colored medallion of some sort, taking up the whole of his little palm.

Doyle frowned as she considered it. "What's that? A brooch?"

Tommy said something unintelligible, and so Doyle reached to lift it, and almost immediately stifled a gasp. Instinctively, she knew that it had belonged to the ghost; it appeared to be some sort of a badge, with a bent hook along the length of its back. Its elaborate, intricately-woven design was inarguably Celtic, and at the center of the design was the stylized figure of a tree.

"Holy *Mother*," she breathed. With growing excitement, she bent to ask, "Where did you find this, Tommy?"

The boy pointed over toward the trees, and said something unintelligible.

Doyle turned to Edward for a translation. "What did he say?"

"He says a man gave it to him."

Doyle lifted her gaze over to the remaining stand of gnarled trees, but there was no man there—and if there had been, she certainly would have noticed, with the boys racing about.

"Michael," she breathed, and then turned to call louder, "Michael—come quickly."

Acton excused himself to the nuns, and walked over to place a fond hand on Edward's head. "Well? Are we ready to go?"

But Doyle was clutching his sleeve, and in her excitement, her words were almost as unintelligible as Tommy's. "No—no, oh, Michael; I've been such a daftie, and small wonder he was that frustrated with me not understandin' what he was tryin' to say.

There's a treasure-trove, Michael—*that's* what he was tryin' to tell me."

"Who? The Viking?" asked her husband quietly, with a warning glance over at the nuns.

Pulling herself together, Doyle continued in a lower tone, "That's why the chieftain was sacrificed—it was the protocol, when they buried their treasure in a sacred grove. *The blood on the roots amplified their power, and the man who died, died well, and would be written of long after his death.*" With a broad smile, she blinked back tears, and gazed over toward the trees. "It's his legacy, Michael."

He stared at her for a long moment, a bit bemused, and so she decided to play her trump card. "Have a look at this." She opened her palm to show him the badge, which Tommy immediately tried to snatch back, being as it appeared his mother was bent on confiscating it.

"Hold a moment, Tommy," his father said, and then he held it between his fingers and examined it closely. "Extraordinary."

With great excitement, Doyle explained, "I had it all wrong, Michael—he wasn't frustrated that we'd dug-up the trees, he was frustrated because we hadn't dug-up *enough* of them—there's treasure to be had." Laughing, she pulled his arm toward the remaining grove. "Come on, let's start diggin'."

"Certainly," he agreed.

CHAPTER 35

With some trepidation, the Heritage representatives walked over to where Doyle and Acton were scrutinizing the ground beneath the trees. "See here, sir," one ventured. "I'm afraid you cannot interfere with official business."

"Here," Doyle called out, as she bent over an exposed tree root. "I think there might be treasure, under here."

"Treasure?" asked Sister Cecelia. "Truly?"

"Have you an extra spade?" Acton asked the representative.

"Sir, I'm afraid we cannot allow—"

"We have spades in the equipment shed," Sister Maria Theresa offered with some excitement. "I'll go fetch them."

"Go help her, Adrian," Doyle directed.

"Now see here," the one representative said, his tone a bit more firm. "We can't have everyone trampin' on the site, willy-nilly."

"If you would give me your probe, please," said Acton, and held out his hand.

Responding to his air of authority, the man handed it over and then watched as Acton bent to probe the area around the ancient root.

"More to the left," Doyle suggested.

"What are you looking for?" asked the librarian, who'd walked over to watch with interest.

"Viking treasure," Doyle told him excitedly. "I think it's buried under here; gold—and, and other things." She paused, and shook her head in bemusement. "Wonderful things—they sorely need to be found."

"*Gersemí.*" The young man said slowly. "It may be the goddess' name, but the word itself means 'treasure.'"

Doyle laughed. "*Now,* you tell me."

He smiled his shy smile. "Sorry."

"No matter—just start diggin'."

Adrian had returned carrying the spades, and the two representatives seemed to have decided to drop all protest, as they began digging alongside Acton and Adrian, with the nuns and the librarian helping to scrape the dirt away with garden trowels, since there weren't enough spades to go around.

Twenty minutes later, their endeavors were interrupted when the Superintendent was seen to cross the courtyard to approach them.

"Chief Inspector," said the Superintendent in a mildly chiding tone; "I'm afraid I cannot allow this; Heritage Ireland has assumed temporary jurisdiction over the site."

"We're Heritage Ireland," one of the representatives disclosed without pausing in his shoveling. "It's all right."

"Here's a spade," Acton said, offering his to the Superintendent. "We think there may be a treasure-trove, buried beneath these roots."

"Oh. Very well," the Pakistani man said, and then removed his suit coat, carefully hanging it on a tree branch before lifting the shovel and joining-in.

Nothing like a treasure hunt, to get everyone on the same team, thought Doyle, as she took the boys to fetch water bottles from the cafeteria.

After they'd excavated a pit that was about three feet deep—progress necessarily slow, in that the hole was laced with the roots of ancient trees—one of the representatives called out. "Here; I've hit somethin' with the probe—just over here."

Adrian stepped over to carefully ply his spade in the area that the man had indicated.

"Nice and slow," the representative cautioned. "We're in no hurry."

The air was palpable with excitement as the others gathered around the rim of the small pit to watch as Adrian and the representative started using their hands to brush away at the hard-packed earth.

"Here's somethin'—careful," said the representative, who could barely contain himself. "Let me use my brush, laddie."

Gradually, the outline of a large, rounded object began to take shape, the dull gold glinting against the dark earth that surrounded it.

"Oh my gosh; I think—I think it's a gold helmet," said the librarian excitedly, as he hovered at the edge. "It looks rather like the one they found at Sutton Hoo."

"Ohhh—will you look at that?" the other representative breathed softly, as Adrian and his fellow representative paused for a moment. The facepiece of a helmet had been exposed, and the echoes of a face—long since dead—seemed to stare up at them from the eye-openings.

The group fell silent, as people do when they are awestruck, and beyond words.

"It's still so bright," whispered Sister Cecilia.

"Gold doesn't corrode," one of the representatives explained in a quiet tone. "It looks exactly the same as when it was buried, over a thousand years ago."

Doyle made to correct him on the date, but was silenced by a warning glance from Acton.

The representative who crouched next to Adrian looked up into the faces lined up above him, and said, almost apologetically, "This is an important find. We really must allow the professionals to take it from here."

"Right," said Acton, who straightened up and directed Adrian, "Let's clear the area and set-up a perimeter." He paused, and then deferred to the Superintendent, "If that meets with your approval."

"It does," the other man agreed happily, his hands on his hips and his shirt wet with sweat.

"Adrian, if you will take the boys to the car, we'll be there shortly."

"Yes, sir," said Adrian, who rose with some reluctance, clearly loath to leave his find.

"Hold, let me take your snap, laddie," the Heritage representative offered. "Just to commemorate the occasion."

"While it's still ours, and before it belongs to everyone else," Sister Maria Theresa agreed with a smile. "I'll take yours, too."

In the sudden flurry of goodwill and picture-taking—even the Superintendent crouched down into the pit to pose—Acton retreated to join his wife, where she leaned against a tree trunk, watching the proceedings. Gently, he touched her arm. "Are you all right?"

She brushed away tears, and confessed, "Yes. No—it's emotional, and hard to explain." She drew a long, shuddering breath. "So much, and so hard to explain."

"An amazing day," he said quietly, as they watched the two nuns clamber down to pose in the pit.

"Aye. An amazin' day."

He drew her against him. "Your ghost meant well by you."

She offered a watery smile. "They always do," she replied. And then corrected, "Well, most of them."

With some sympathy, he rested his head against hers. "It can't be easy, being you."

"Fah, husband; I could say the same about you. It's that ying and yams thing again; I've smoothed you down a bit, and you've made me miles braver—mainly because I've had to be, due to the aforementioned smoothin'-down. I used to be like that nervous little librarian, hidin' away in the upper stacks, but now he's been thrust into the spotlight, will-he or nil-he—same as what happened to me."

"Time to clear out," announced one of the Heritage representatives. "It's been a pleasure, everyone. If you would coordinate all media appearances through our office, it would be greatly appreciated—we should try to show the public that Heritage Ireland is worth our tithe."

Reminded, Doyle turned to ask her husband in a low tone, "Where's the badge? Do we have to turn it in?"

"I vote no," he replied easily. "I imagine it was intended for you."

"No, it was intended for Tommy," Doyle corrected him with a smile. "But I'll keep it for him, 'til he's old enough."

CHAPTER 36

And so, yet again, Doyle found herself at a formal outdoor gathering behind St. Brigid's School for Girls, pinning on her publicity-photo smile for the media photographers. There were many more besides Robbie O'Shaughnessy, this time around, what with the archeological find attracting the entire world's attention.

Doyle paused in the festivities to gaze up the school's back wall, deciding—strangely enough—that it didn't seems as familiar as it used to be. It was a part of her past, now—when for so long it had been her immediate and certain present—and she felt a pang of nostalgia. Time moved on, and nothing stayed the same, no matter how much we clung to the hope that it would. I suppose I'm truly a Londoner, now, she thought, and inwardly winced. Shame on me; my mother would be that gobsmacked.

Acton came over. "How are you holding up?"

"I'm longin' to go home," she confessed.

With some sympathy, he disclosed, "Not just yet, I'm afraid.

I've sent for my solicitors and Layton—there will be a series of meetings to set-up."

Layton was his banker in London, and she sighed. "Can't the school buy their new property without us, husband?"

"The meetings will concern the historical site because at present, I own the land."

She blinked. "You *do*? How is that?"

"It was an arrangement so that the school could move out from under its debt; they leased the property from me for a nominal sum."

She stared at him for a moment, and then couldn't help laughing. "Holy *Mother*, Michael—you've fallen headlong into another giant vat of money. How on earth d'you manage it?"

He smiled. "I can deed the property back, now—the school should become self-sustaining, if a museum site is constructed."

"With a charitable foundation," she guessed.

"Yes. This one aboveboard."

Bemused, she gazed back over the crowd. "Ironic, is what it is; after my fine speech about steppin' into the future, the school will instead take a step backward into the past."

But he insisted, "The science-lab will become a reality— certainly the school will now be able to afford to purchase the adjacent property. Indeed, the orphanage would benefit from a larger footprint, and so perhaps the lab could take its place, with a new orphanage being built near door."

She smiled, since he'd clearly been busy making plans—a much better use of his talents than the usual masterminding. "A good thing Javid will paint her portrait, then—the school is goin' to be unrecognizable, soon. Not to mention it's goin' to be famous, in all the history books. Who'd have thought it, back when the nuns were runnin' it on a shoe-string?"

"Indeed."

She glanced up at him. "'Tis a good lesson, Michael. Some legacies are miles more important than other legacies—no matter how much you think you've a handle on such things. St. Brigid's will now be remembered as a Viking trove, but I'd argue that its true legacy is the little girls who've passed through here, the better for having done so."

Again, she looked up at the school's back wall, the same as she'd done a million times before, and the same as so many other nameless little girls had done. "You might be dazzled by Viking gold, but the most important legacy of all is the one you pass on to the children."

"A very good point," he said, and leaned to kiss her temple.

She insisted, "'Tis true, Michael. All this nonsense about storytellers tellin' their stupid sagas about mighty warriors, when the even the poorest peasant knows that what you pass on to your children is the only legacy that truly matters. That's the surest and best way to achieve immortality."

"Paddycake," Tommy shouted, as he ran up to them with his hands raised.

"Your turn," they both hastily disclaimed in unison.

Printed in Great Britain
by Amazon

30423152R00142